FAMILIAR THINGS

FAMILIAR

HWANG
SOK-YONG

THINGS

SCRIBE
Melbourne • London

Translated by
Sora Kim-Russell

Scribe Publications
18–20 Edward St, Brunswick, Victoria 3065, Australia
2 John St, Clerkenwell, London, WC1N 2ES, United Kingdom

First published in Korean as *Natikeun Sesang* by Munhakdongne 2011
First published in English by Scribe 2017

Typeset in 11.65/17.15 pt Adobe Garamond by the publishers
Printed and bound in China by 1010 Printing Co Ltd

Scribe Publications is committed to the sustainable use of natural resources and the use of paper products made responsibly from those resources.

This book is published with the support of the
Literature Translation Institute of Korea (LTI Korea)

LTI Korea
Literature Translation Institute of Korea

9781925322019 (Australian edition)
9781925228991 (UK edition)
9781925548051 (e-book)

CiP entries for this title are available from the National Library of Australia and the British Library

scribepublications.com.au
scribepublications.co.uk

1

The sun was sinking toward the edge of the fields on the other side of the river. In the brief time it took to glance away and look back again, the enormous and perfectly round sun had already fallen headlong below the horizon. The truck raced down the riverside expressway, past the outskirts of the city, but as soon as the bridge came into sight, traffic began to back up, and the truck inched its way forward.

The boy rode standing in the back of the truck, facing forward, both hands gripping the metal frame right behind the driver's seat, so he had a clear view of the river alongside and the road ahead. He had boarded the garbage truck with his mother on the eastern end of the big city. The slow line of trucks came to a halt, crept forward, and came to a halt again as they made their way off the expressway and onto an unpaved road that skirted an island in the river. The unpaved road ran alongside a stream that branched off the river before rejoining it at the other end of the island. Only the western sky was still aglow; everything else was turning dark. Standing with its back to the northern hills on the opposite side of the stream was a small village. Cozy lights twinkled in every window. The boy thought one of those houses was surely meant for him and his mother.

The tall silver grass swaying on the banks of the stream in the dusky light made it seem like they had suddenly arrived at a foreign, faraway land. As the trucks began to flick on their headlights, the vehicles were swallowed up by clouds of dust. The road curved away from the village with its warm lights, and the trucks began to climb uphill; something like grains of wheat or rice plinked off their faces in the dark. There were three men and two women, in addition to the boy and his mother, who had climbed up onto the full load of trash in the back of the truck at the waste-collection site in the city. Everyone had a decent-sized scrap of plastic to sit on or to wrap around their legs as they stood and clung to the sides of the truck. They'd been surrounded by garbage since the start of the ride, so they didn't notice the strange new odours coming at them. But as soon as the truck crested the hill and stopped in a spacious lot at the top, they could barely breathe from the stench. The smell was unbearably foul, a vile combination of every bad odour in the world—manure, sewage, spoiled food, hard-boiled soy sauce, fermented soybean paste. Clinging to their faces and forearms and clothing in the dark, boldly alighting on the corners of their mouths and eyes, and probing at them with cold, sticky tongues were swarms of flies.

The boy knew better than to tell other people his real name. Least of all his family name. The sort of kids who went to school liked to call each other by their full names, but as far as he was concerned that was strictly for elementary-school babies. He had turned thirteen that year, but whenever he was out prowling the alleys, he added two years and said he was fifteen. Once, the older boys in his neighbourhood ganged up on him and tried to pull his pants down so they could check him for pubic hair as proof of his age. He headbutted one of them in the face and broke the boy's front tooth. They, in turn, left him bleeding from both nostrils, and must have busted one of his ribs as well, because his whole chest ached and smarted with each inhale and exhale for a month after. But what mattered was that he'd kept his dignity. The kids in the alleys each had a different name for him: Hopper, Stork, Bugeye. Hopper, short for grasshopper, because his fourth grade homeroom teacher had said he had long arms and legs and ran as fast as one; and Stork, instead of the more dignified Heron or Crane, which also had long legs and a spindly neck. He didn't care for those names, but he thought the nickname Bugeye wasn't too shabby. He'd been given that nickname by a police officer back where he used to live. One day, he and some other boys were having fun smashing in the windows of the police station. They got caught while trying to run away, and were made to kneel down in front of the police officer to await their punishment. The officer smacked Bugeye on the head over and over with a rolled-up wad of police reports, and christened him. *Don't you dare roll your eyes at me, you bug-eyed little punk! I'll pop them right out of their sockets! Get your father in here, bug-eyes!* After that, whenever one of his buddies tried to call him by another name, he beat the hell out of them, but when they called him Bugeye, he didn't get angry and sometimes even deigned to respond, and soon took to introducing himself by that name whenever he met other kids his age. He took on the name to distinguish himself from kids from decent families who lived in fancy apartment buildings, but he had also earned it, the same way grown-ups earned a badge with each new stint in the slammer.

Bugeye had quit school halfway through the fifth grade. His mother was a street vendor who made just enough to put three meals a day on the table and to pay the rent on their cramped room in the hillside slum. He used to loaf around in the alleyways with other boys his age, but at some point he'd started going with his mother to the market so he could pick up a little work of his own at one of the clothing stalls. The stalls were inside a nice-looking building right on the main road, but crowded together out of sight in the back alley were small sweatshops; the owners each rented one of those cramped workspaces where they employed a handful of workers at a few sewing machines. Bugeye's job was to run back and forth, supplying fabric, thread, buttons, and other materials to the workers in the sweatshops in back, and delivering the completed merchandise to the clothing stalls out front. One day, just as evening was falling, he headed back to the spot where his mother usually laid out her goods. The other women were packing up for the day, but his mother wasn't there.

'Where'd my mum go?'

One of the women cackled and said, 'She must be getting some on the side.'

'I think your dad's back,' the woman next to her explained.

'My dad?'

The women pointed in the direction of the food alley. Bugeye searched up and down the alley, which was heavy with the smells of fish grilling and blood-sausage soup boiling. He peeked into every restaurant on both sides until he spotted his mother sitting across a table from some man. The man had his back turned, making it impossible to make out his face, but he wore an army field jacket and a blue baseball cap. Bugeye hesitantly tiptoed inside. His mother saw him and waved him over. Bugeye walked over to the table and was about to check whether it really was his dad when the man turned around and tried to pat Bugeye on the head. Bugeye titled his head back and darted out of reach. It was not his dad. The man awkwardly retrieved his hand.

'Look how big you are. Seems like only yesterday you were learning how to walk …'

'Say hello,' his mother said. 'This is a friend of your dad's.'

Bugeye gave the man a curt nod, sat down next to his mother, and coolly perused him. He had big, bright eyes and a big nose, which made him look friendly enough, but a huge, blue birthmark covered almost the entire left side of his face, from just below his eye to down across his cheek. Where had Bugeye seen that before? Of course! Half-white, half-blue face. Long pointy chin. Half-red, half-blue cape. It was none other than Baron Ashura from *Mazinger Z*. The villain and right-hand man of Dr. Hell, who was always cooking up some evil plan despite being constantly foiled by Mazinger Z, robot defender of good. Bugeye's fists clenched, the urge to fight blazed up inside him, and he glared at the blue-faced man.

'It's just a shack, but you won't have to pay rent. You'll make three times what you make now. Where else are you going to find a deal like that?'

The man continued where he had left off when Bugeye arrived. His mother nodded and leaned in closer, her face eager.

'I don't know when his dad will get out,' she said

hesitantly. 'If you can get us registered, I'll do whatever it takes.'

The man glanced over at Bugeye, who was still glaring at him with his clenched fists ready on the table, and asked, 'How old are you?'

Bugeye couldn't very well tell him he was fifteen, with his mother sitting right there, so he kept his mouth shut.

'Thirteen,' she answered for him.

The man's jaw dropped open in exaggerated surprise.

'What? Awful big for thirteen, aren't you? If anyone asks, you're fifteen.'

Bugeye hid his sudden delight and muttered bashfully, 'All of my friends are fifteen ...'

'Good, good. We'll say you finished middle school.' He turned back to Bugeye's mother. 'I'll register you with the city so you can work on the first line. If the boy helps with the sorting on the second line, then between the two of you, you'll make double what others do.'

That night, Bugeye could tell his mother was too excited to sleep.

'I've been worried sick ever since the landlord told us we had to get out, but this is good. Now we've got work and a place to stay. What a relief.'

Bugeye's mother and father had grown up in an orphanage together. At some point, his father ran away by himself and drifted around the city for a while before ending up on one of the work crews that had been formed in every district in the city. Though he wasn't able to save enough to become a proper junk man on his own, he was put in charge of collecting recyclables for a small area. It was around then that Bugeye's dad went back for his mother. She was grown by then, still living in the orphanage and looking after children who were barely out of nappies.

The problem with collecting discarded items was that many of the items were still in perfectly good condition, and sometimes the trash collectors were even asked to hold onto stolen goods until they could be sold, and so they often found themselves accused of being thieves. Whenever there were increased reports of thefts, the trash collectors were called into the police station at all hours of the day, and the police would even order whoever was in charge of an area to choose a worker to take the blame. Trash collectors who had already done time once or twice before would volunteer to go back to prison, and once they'd done time, stealing the iron gates off houses or taking expensive copper or aluminium from construction sites didn't seem like such a big deal. Not to mention, while collecting discarded items in residential areas, they could sniff out empty houses to break into later.

Bugeye's father went missing the year Bugeye dropped out of school. Actually, Bugeye had been more or less forced to quit: with his father gone, money grew tight at home. It wasn't the first time Bugeye's father had disappeared, so Bugeye and his mother waited a couple of weeks, thinking he had been caught in yet another of the cops' dragnets. They assumed someone from the police station or district precinct would call them in as usual and tell them that a certain someone had been arrested and was being held somewhere; but this time, to their surprise, there was no news at all, and instead one of the young men who had worked with his father tipped off Bugeye's mother. He told her that Bugeye's father had been taken away and thrown into a re-education camp. Ever since the new general had seized power and declared that he would clean up society, rumours had been going around that gangsters, ex-cons, and general hoodlums, as well as anyone who even so much as had a tattoo that made ordinary people feel anxious or who otherwise created a sense of disharmony in their environment, regardless of how old or young they were, were being rounded up and sent away for a period of re-education in order to turn them into new people. Scores of people disappeared and were said to be undergoing rehabilitation at re-education camps installed in army bases around the country.

Bugeye's family had never lived high on the hog, but at least they'd never gone hungry. Now, Bugeye and his mother had to scramble all day just to earn their three meals. Even when he had been in school, he was sometimes teased by the apartment building boys who called him a garbage-eating bum, and each time that happened, he had used those long, swift limbs of his to beat the living hell out of them.

'Come on, we haven't got all day.'

The driver rolled down the window and urged everyone off the truck. People passed their belongings to each other and carefully clambered down from the pile of garbage. Bugeye and his mother dragged down a bundle of bedding, a large plastic tote, and a basin containing pots and pans and the like that they had selected and brought from their old place. The driver revved the engine, spewing out a plume of foul-smelling exhaust, to make them get a move on. When they stepped off the truck, astronauts appeared from out of the darkness. They wore boots and hardhats, caps with headlamps attached to their foreheads like miners, thick rubber gloves, and large masks. One of the astronauts came toward them and pulled off his mask, but neither of them recognised who it was at first.

'Hey, it's me. Let's go.'

When his mother heard the man's voice, she took Bugeye by the hand. It was Baron Ashura. He hoisted their bedding onto his shoulder as though it weighed nothing, and took the lead, the plastic tote gripped in his other hand, while Bugeye and his mother each took one side of the basin that contained the rest of their meagre belongings and followed. Lights blinked drowsily at the base of the mountain of garbage where a row of trucks made its way up amid a growl of engines and a storm of dust.

As they got closer, Bugeye discovered that the blinking lights were coming from shanty huts of different shapes and sizes. There were canvas tents, rough structures made from wooden boards haphazardly nailed together and wrapped in plastic, and walls constructed out of random store signs and cardboard boxes. The shacks stretched on endlessly into the dark, with hardly enough space for a person to squeeze in between them. The rows of shacks were divided by paths no wider across than a single car lane. Judging from the light spilling out of every plastic window in the squat shacks, there were people living in each of them. In small lots that had been left empty here and there among the shacks, men were gathered around bonfires, boiling or grilling food over the flames, and drinking *soju* and *makkolli*. The Baron introduced Bugeye and his mother to the men in one of the empty lots.

'This woman is like a sister to me. She's registered with the city now, so let's treat her like family.'

'Oh great, just what we need, more competition,' one of the men grumbled, his face set in a frown. He had just placed a tin can on top of the fire and had squatted down to blow on the cinders.

The men all ignored Bugeye, who was standing behind his mother and the Baron. As any good crew leader would, the Baron repeated the fact that she had every right to be there, his tone making it clear that it was not up for discussion.

'We've already got forty-five people registered to our sector.'

'We're finding less and less stuff worth selling. It's a real problem.'

'There'll be sunny days and there'll be rainy days,' the Baron assured them. 'Now, who's going to lend a hand? Whoever helps, the soju's on me.'

'The old plasterer's shack ought to be empty.'

'That was three, four days ago. When I took a look at it earlier, all the usable stuff had already been scavenged.'

Bugeye and his mother followed the three men to the empty shack: everything had been stripped away and carried off, except for the foundation. Someone had even pulled up the vinyl sheeting used to cover the ground, but pieces of cardboard from torn-up boxes that had been spread underneath the vinyl were still there, damp from the bare earth. One of the men lifted up the cardboard.

'Look at this—they forgot to take the Styrofoam.'

'Let's move all this crap over there and build a shack right up against mine.'

The two men whispered and cackled.

'Old bachelor's gotta keep his sister close, huh?'

The Baron pretended not to hear them.

'This'll do. We just need to lay down new cardboard and cover it with some linoleum. Shouldn't take more than an hour.'

Bugeye and his mother followed Baron Ashura down

the slope to the end of the row of shanties. It was a decent-looking spot, a short distance from the neighbouring sector and far enough from the road where the trucks made their way up and down the hill of garbage. While the three men were off gathering materials for their new place, Bugeye and his mother put their things down and squatted next to the Baron's shack.

'I thought we were moving to the country,' Bugeye complained.

His mother sighed.

'People live here, just like anywhere else,' she said.

'People? All I see are flies and garbage. It stinks.'

'It may be garbage now, but they say it turns to gold,' his mother said playfully.

At first, all Bugeye could see were shadowy mounds in the dark, but he couldn't tell what they were. The three men caused a racket as they took turns dragging a cart full of scraps to the shack. Everything had come out of the landfill: wooden beams of different lengths, crates and scraps of plastic from the fish market, plastic tarps of all shapes and colours from street food carts, black felted fabric that had been used in greenhouses, linoleum flooring in all possible patterns. All at once, the area around the shack turned into a construction site, and people poured out of neighbouring shacks to lend a hand. Under the Baron's command, wooden beams were cut or fixed together to form pillars and planted upright, while others were angled against the pillars to form buttresses. Fish crates were pulled apart with hammers, and the boards nailed together to form walls. The insides of the walls were lined with plastic, then Styrofoam, then a tight, even layer of cardboard. To make the floor, they first spread a plastic tarp on the bare ground, then more Styrofoam, then cardboard from the pulled-apart boxes, and then the linoleum. For the roof, they covered boards with Styrofoam and sheets of cardboard, on top of which went the black felted material and linoleum, followed by a frame of four-by-twos nailed in place to make sure the roof didn't fly off. For the final touch, they draped the food cart tent over the roof to complete the thirteen-square-metre shack. Since it was right up against the Baron's shack, it looked much larger than the others from the front, like a single house. Baron Ashura stuck a candle on a flat piece of stone to light the room. Bugeye's mother pulled an old shirt from their belongings and went to work scrubbing the linoleum. The floral print that slowly emerged in the flickering light of the candle looked colourful and vibrant.

'Goodness, it's like magic. All we need is a camp stove and we'll have a kitchen, too.'

Bugeye's mother kept gazing around at the room in wonder. The Baron shook his head, the candlelight making his blue birthmark look all the more dramatic, and said, 'Don't worry about it. We got all that stuff. Now it's time to celebrate.'

When they returned to the bonfire, the Baron handed several bills to one of the men who had helped.

'Go get some instant ramen and several bottles of soju.'

On top of a makeshift stove fashioned from an oil drum sawed in half, something was boiling away and smelling delicious.

'What's cooking?' the Baron asked a man who wore a hard hat perched at a stylish angle on his head.

'Flower Island trough stew, what else? With extra chilli powder. It'll hit the spot.'

Soon enough, the younger man who had run to the store returned with a plastic bag. The Baron ripped open the ramen wrapper and shook the packet of powdered broth into the pot. He was about to add the dried noodles when Hard Hat stopped him.

'Brother, noodles go in last. Gotta eat the good stuff first.'

'We scored big today,' Baron Ashura said. 'This looks like real ham from the Co-op's sector.'

'Sure, it pays to help each other out,' one of the men said. 'You should go independent, too. Start your own operation.'

'You got any idea how expensive the permit fee is for a private truck sector?' Hard Hat said.

The Baron added with a sour look on his face, 'And we don't have the right connections anyway.'

'The district dumps have nothing good. The private

sectors get the best stuff.'

Hard Hat pulled a warped spoon out of his shirt pocket, wiped it a few times on his sleeve, and had a taste of the soup.

'Damn, that's good.'

The Baron scooped some ham and sausage into a small scorched and dented pot, and gave it to Bugeye and his mother.

'Our new family members are the guests of honour today. Eat up.'

Bugeye's mother took a hesitant sip of the soup and whispered to Bugeye, 'It tastes just like army-base stew.'

Bugeye popped a sausage in his mouth and started wolfing down the soup, his spoon clinking against his mother's as they rushed to eat their fill. The men sliced off the tops of tiny plastic bottles of drinking yogurt that they'd scavenged from the trash, shook out the dirt or scum inside, and used them as shot glasses for the soju. As the smell of food spread, flies came swarming. The flies landed on the food the second it was fished out of the broth, and rode it during the short trip from bowl to mouth; when the mouths tried to shoo them away, the flies merely fluttered their wings. Some of the flies clung to the food as it went into the mouths, and only buzzed off when they felt the tip of a tongue.

'Suckers are still feisty.'

'They're usually slower at night, but I guess the fire

warmed them up.'

'I thought once summer was over, they'd be gone, too. At this rate they'll be sticking around until the Chuseok holiday.'

'It's fine, it'll put hair on your chest. We must've eaten a whole pint of flies this summer.'

Bugeye shooed them as he ate, but he still ended up choking on a fly that had drowned in the soup. The Baron gave Bugeye and his mother some of the ramen noodles the men had boiled in the remaining broth.

'If you want to be a real worker,' he told Bugeye's mother, 'you first have to learn how to get by on this.'

*

While the grown-ups poured each other shot after shot of soju, Bugeye snuck away from the fireside and returned to their new shack. His mother stayed with Baron Ashura to learn more about how things worked there. Once Bugeye had struck a match, lit a candle, and lain down on the slick linoleum, the place felt much roomier and more comfortable than where they used to live. Just then, he thought he saw someone poke the top of their head through the door and steal a peek at him, but when he looked up, the head disappeared. Bugeye sat up and waited, his eyes fixed on the door. Sure enough, before long, the impatient head poked in again.

'Who are you?' he called out.

The half-hidden head shook with giggles but did not answer. When Bugeye scooted closer to the door, the source of the giggles burst out from behind it. It was a boy, much younger-looking than Bugeye. The boy wore a torn baseball cap cocked to one side, a sleeveless undershirt, and baggy oversized jeans that had been hacked off at the knee to fit him.

'Who the hell are you?' Bugeye asked.

'Who the hell are *you*?' the boy said, and let out a funny, high-pitched giggle.

Annoyed, Bugeye snatched the boy's cap off. It was embroidered with small letters that spelled out *Middle School Baseball*, and the back of the too-large cap had been folded and sewn together to fit.

'Give it back! C'mon, give it!'

Bugeye hid the cap behind him with one hand and reached the other forward to rub his knuckles on the boy's head, to give him a noogie, when he saw that the left half of his head was completely hairless. The scalp looked wrinkled. The boy charged into the room with his shoes on, so Bugeye threw the cap out the door and stepped outside. The boy ran to pick up the cap. He put it back on and spat on the ground.

'Fucker,' he muttered.

'Hey, I'm sorry!' Bugeye said. 'Where do you live?'

'There.' The boy stuck out his bottom lip and used it to

point at the shack next door.

'You're related to the Baron—I mean, to the crew leader?'

The boy nodded, and then reeled off one answer after another to questions Bugeye had not asked.

'He's my dad, I don't have a mum, it's just the two of us, Dad doesn't talk to me.'

'Why not?'

The boy hung his head.

'He says I'm too stupid.'

The boy did seem a little slow, but Bugeye figured, if this was Baron Ashura's son, then he'd better make a point of getting on his good side. Bugeye held up his hand and signalled to the boy to wait. He rummaged through the tin cookie box he used to store his most treasured possessions in, and pulled out his Mazinger Z action figure.

'Here, you can have this. It's the most powerful robot in the world.'

To Bugeye, the toy was just something he kept for old time's sake. He'd have lost face if he ever showed it to his friends back home. The plastic joints were a little loose, but the metal springs that fired the arm and leg missiles were still tightly coiled. It was one of several discarded toys his father had saved from a scrapheap one day. There was the robot, a racing car, and some wooden blocks for building toy houses; that day, Bugeye had received all of those gifts, and a banana, to boot.

'Look, if you push here …'

Bugeye pressed a button on the arm, and the fist shot out. The boy stamped his feet and giggled with joy. Bugeye picked up the plastic fist, fitted it back into the socket, and handed it to the boy.

'What's your name?'

'Baldspot.'

'Baldspot? What kind of a name is that?'

Despite the unusual name, Bugeye took an instant liking to the kid. He felt reassured to know that people here went by nicknames just as they did in the hillside slums in the city.

'How old are you?'

The boy spread all ten fingers in Bugeye's face. Bugeye was taken aback. How could they only be three years apart in age?

Baldspot poked Bugeye in the chest and asked, 'What's *your* name?'

'Bugeye.'

'Bugeye!' he exclaimed, letting out another high-pitched giggle. 'Buggy-buggy-Bugeye!'

The boy bent over with laughter until his head was practically touching the ground. Then he gestured for Bugeye to follow him, and started to scuttle away.

'Hey,' Bugeye said, hanging back. 'Where're you going?'

Baldspot turned and pressed a finger to his lips.

'It's top secret,' he whispered. 'If Dad or the other grown-ups find out, we'll get in trouble.'

'Then you better tell me where we're going first.'

'Just follow me.'

Bugeye followed Baldspot down the path lined with slapped-together shacks of all shapes and colours. He'd heard there were some two thousand households altogether living on the island, but he was still amazed to see how the rows of shanties not only filled the flat areas but even extended all the way up the slopes of the hill. Candlelight seeped faintly out of each diminutive plastic window. They came across a few other empty lots where adults were passing drinks around and children were running in and out of the rows like they were playing hide-and-go-seek. The two marched briskly over the hill that marked the edge of the shantytown. The wet grass was cool against their ankles. Bugeye knew what the island was called; he'd heard the name of it when he and his mother were leaving the waste-collection site back in the city. When he first heard the name 'Flower Island', he thought they were going to some paradise overlooking the ocean.

Bugeye and Baldspot made their way over the hill of garbage and out of the shantytown; there, they arrived on the western outskirts of the triangular island. As soon as they crested the hill, they were looking down on the river. The river itself was swallowed up by the dark, but the passing headlights of cars racing down the highway bounced off the surface of the water and made it shimmer.

'What're you doing? Hurry up.'

Baldspot nudged Bugeye away from where he stood, transfixed by the river. They seemed to be walking through a vegetable patch; something kept catching on Bugeye's ankles and tripping him up. Baldspot came to an abrupt stop on a sandy hill where tall willows, silver grass, and cattails stirred in the wind. Bugeye looked around. Far off to the east was a brightly lit bridge. He remembered that the truck they arrived in had taken a left-hand turn onto Flower Island immediately after crossing that bridge. Towering over the river on a raised area at the centre of the triangular island, and higher and longer across than the hill they stood on, was a mountain of garbage. Work hours were over, so there were no trucks in sight. Baldspot squatted down and groped around in the sand: a rope appeared, and he gave it a tug.

'There's one on your side, too,' he said.

Bugeye reached down and found an identical rope attached to a four-by-two sticking out of the sand. When they pulled on their ropes at the same time, two posts rose up straight and tall as a canvas roof was pulled tautly into place. Baldspot picked up a plastic bag that had been stashed under the roof, pulled out a match, and lit a candle. Thick pieces of cardboard covered by a large scrap of blue-and-white-striped tarp formed a floor, and there were even low walls on either side built from cinder blocks. Dug from the side of the sandy hill and open to the river, looking just like someone had taken a bite out

22

of a bun, was a neat little hideout.

'This is our headquarters,' Baldspot said proudly. He placed the Mazinger Z robot in a box inside the hideout. Bugeye kept patting the cinder blocks in amazement.

'It's just like a house,' he said.

'Yep!' Baldspot copied Bugeye, and gave the wall a pat, too.

Bugeye later learned from the other kids that the place used to be an army guard post. The boys of the landfill had carried pieces of cardboard and scraps of tarp over from the garbage and transformed it into a cozy room. They had even installed the canvas awning so they would have shade on sunny days and shelter on rainy days. The awning doubled as camouflage simply by lowering the ropes and covering the site up when it was not in use. Each time the awning rose, it was like a stage curtain sweeping open to reveal a new world. When they sat inside and looked out, the view was completely different from when they were just standing on top of the sandy hill. The shadows of silver grass and willow trees stood tall in one corner of the rectangular frame created by the cinderblock walls and canvas awning, and the broad expanse of the river flowed through the middle; on the surface of that river, moonlight glimmered, and the lights of the city glowed faintly in the distance on the far side of the water.

'So, this is your headquarters,' said Bugeye, unable to hide his amazement and envy.

'I'll get in trouble if our captain finds out,' Baldspot mumbled. He pulled a big stack of magazines out of the drawer of a squat table in the far corner. The little guy seemed more proud than afraid to show Bugeye the magazines. Bugeye was already familiar with them, having been shown the same kind of thing by the older boys in the hillside slums. They were adult magazines from some foreign country, filled cover to cover with pictures of naked people.

'Who's your captain?'

'Mole. He's scary.'

'How old is he?'

'I don't know. He's practically a grown-up. Bigger than you. Good worker.'

Bugeye and Baldspot sat with their legs drawn up, chins on knees, and looked out at the river for a long while. Bugeye liked the fact that Baldspot didn't say much unless he was spoken to. But despite sounding slow, he seemed to pick up on things pretty fast. Maybe he was deeper than he looked. Being teased and picked on by other kids had a way of deepening a person. Before he'd learned to fight back, Bugeye, too, had been a quiet kid who kept to himself.

'Do you like it here?' Bugeye asked him.

Baldspot nodded emphatically.

'Do you come here during the day, too?'

'I come here whenever I want. The other boys come in the evening.'

Bugeye hesitated for a moment before asking, 'Hey, listen … Is your dad nice?'

'I don't know. He doesn't talk to me.'

'Thing is, me and my mum are supposed to work for your dad starting tomorrow …'

'Kids aren't supposed to work here. I think you and Mole are the only ones who can,' Baldspot mumbled. He suddenly started to giggle, and then he blurted out, 'My dad might stick it in your mum!'

Bugeye socked Baldspot right on top of his baseball cap. Baldspot fell to one side and yelled like he was dying.

'Don't hit me on the head, fucker!'

'You asked for it! You talked shit about my mum!'

Baldspot rubbed his head with both hands and inched away, dragging his bum in the sand.

'I don't have a mum, and you don't have a dad. Some woman lived with us before, but she left.'

'I have a dad, you idiot. People don't just live with other people like that.'

'They do here.' Baldspot readjusted his cap. 'My mum spilled hot water on my head when I was little, and that's why I'm not smart, so don't hit me on the head!'

'Okay, okay, I won't hit you on the head. Let's come back tomorrow.'

They blew out the candle, pulled down the awning to conceal the hideout, and headed back the way they'd come. When they were halfway across the field, Baldspot squatted down and dug up a handful of something. He offered it to Bugeye.

'Try it. It's good.'

Bugeye brushed the dirt off and rolled the thing around in his hands until he realised it was a peanut. They were standing in the middle of a peanut field. He cracked open the shell and felt the soft meat inside.

'We'll get in trouble if we're caught,' Baldspot said with his funny giggle.

'Whose field is this?'

'A bunch of farmers live over there, in the village across the stream. The fields belong to them.'

They had passed the field and were climbing the hill at the edge of the shantytown when Baldspot suddenly tapped Bugeye on the arm and hit the deck. Startled, Bugeye followed suit and lay down on his stomach, but he didn't see anything or hear any voices. Bugeye hesitantly started to stand back up again.

'There's nothing there,' he grumbled.

'Shh,' said Baldspot, pulling him down by the scruff of his neck. 'Hold still a bit.'

Bugeye didn't know what was going on, but he lay with his back against the wet grass, waiting. After a long while, Baldspot got up; Bugeye got up, too, and looked around. All he could hear was adults off in the distance, shouting and singing and arguing loudly with each other. Baldspot stared hard at a spot in the darkness.

'They're gone now,' he said.

'Who's gone?'

'I'm the only one who sees them.'

It occurred to Bugeye that Baldspot might have just been messing with him.

'Shit, you trying to convince me you saw a ghost or something?' he grumbled.

'They look like blue lights,' Baldspot said as he headed up the hill. 'And I'm the only one who knows about them.'

Suddenly spooked, Bugeye ran up the hill ahead of Baldspot. When he got to the top, he found himself facing the lights of the shantytown and the shadowy mounds of garbage.

*

Bugeye heard indistinct chatter around him in his sleep, but decided to stay curled up and ignore it.

'Wake up, honey,' his mother said, pulling the blanket off him. 'It's time to go to work.'

She shook Bugeye, who managed to sit up but still had his eyes closed, and then stood him up by both arms.

'Aren't you old enough to dress yourself by now?'

While Bugeye stumbled around, shoving his legs into pants and pulling on a long-sleeved shirt, his mother was busy turning herself into a space alien: half of her face was covered with a cloth mask, and she wore a floppy hat with a wide, round brim. Underneath the hat, which was the type that farm women wore while weeding fields, she had wrapped a kerchief around her head. On her hands she wore a double layer of cloth work gloves topped with sturdy rubber gloves. She carried a pitchfork the length of her arm. With boots that came all the way up to her knees, the whole get-up made her look like she was on her way to dig for clams. From out of nowhere, she produced a torn army cap, cloth work gloves, and rubber gloves for Bugeye, as well as a pair of combat boots with the toes so worn-down they'd turned white.

'Our crew leader got all of this for you. Now hurry up!' she said, her voice muffled by the mask.

The cap was so big that it slid down until the rim touched his nose, and the combat boots were so huge that he had plenty of space left in the toes and heels, but the thought that he was becoming a worker today, equal to the grown-ups, made him feel proud. He put on the double layer of gloves, just like his mother's, and picked up the other pitchfork. Two long baskets with shoulder straps were waiting for them outside. His mother hoisted one of the baskets onto her back first, and Bugeye followed suit: with the basket strapped to his back, he felt he'd instantly grown several inches taller. The main path through the shantytown was already jammed with other people dressed just like them. The crowd pushed on to the clearing in the dumpsite where the trucks turned around, and then everyone quickly dispersed. It seemed they all knew exactly where they were supposed to be.

'Took you two long enough!'

Baron Ashura made his way toward them against the flow of people, and put his hand on Bugeye's mother's shoulder.

'I'm sorry,' she said. 'The path was so crowded ...'

'It's fine. Now then, you see those two mounds?'

'I see four.'

'No, no, just the big ones. On the right is the district sector, and on the left is the private sector. We go to the right.'

Other than a quick glance up and down, the Baron acted like Bugeye wasn't even there. He was probably thinking, Thank goodness the basket wasn't dragging on the ground at least. The towering mounds were filled with all variety of discarded things. After the trash pickers had gone over the pile and picked out whatever they could, a bulldozer came along to flatten down what remained. As they worked, the trash pickers' legs sank deeper and their feet caught on things, and sometimes objects clung to their boots and only let go after a shake or two. When they reached the top of the mound, they could see the riverside expressway and its line of trucks with their headlights on, crawling over the bridge onto Flower Island. Clouds of dust billowed in the glow of the headlights. The leaders for each district sector called out to their work teams.

'All right! Double file! Get a move on!'

The Baron explained that from five to nine in the morning was the busiest, as that was when the best items could be found. The next batch came in at noon, and the last batch came in the evening, which meant they would be at it for over twelve hours every day. The workers stood with their districts and waited for the garbage truck marked with their district number to pull in. The ones in front were those who had paid the permit fee and were officially registered to work on the first line. After they'd fished out the best items, the second-line workers were allowed to go through whatever was left. The Baron gave Bugeye's mother tip after tip.

'Whoever snags it first, it's theirs. Understand? Plastic containers and anything made from thin plastic comes later. Most important is linoleum, tarp, and anything made from thick plastic. If it's metal, grab it. Glass bottles, grab it. As for clothes or rags or other fabric, unless it's in good shape, skip it. Paper comes first.'

The Baron had tips for Bugeye, too.

'You're supposed to be in the second line, but stay right behind your mother, and grab whatever she misses. If her basket gets full, go empty it for her and bring it back.'

The garbage trucks began to file in. The garbage that arrived early in the morning was mostly from the downtown and commercial areas, so it contained the best items. The residential-area and apartment-complex trash came in around noon, and the waste from nearby construction sites and factories came later. The trucks with their headlights beaming crawled single-file up the hill, illuminating the black swarms of flies that buzzed around in the dust clouds. The crew leader of another unit who'd been checking the district numbers printed under the driver's side windows called out, and one of the trash pickers swiftly ran forward and guided the truck like a traffic cop to the spot where his unit would be working that day. The driver circled around and backed into place as the man shouted, 'A little further, a little further!' The truck stopped, and the bed of the truck began to lift. Garbage poured out, and the pickers from that unit raced toward the pile. More trucks kept pulling into the dumpsite.

The Baron called out to his unit, 'Here comes our truck!'

Hard Hat ran ahead to guide the truck, and the rest of the pickers chased after it as it drove past. The truck turned around and dumped the garbage as other trucks from the same district poured in. The trash pickers instantly dove into the pile, causing one of the trucks that had been backing up to hit the brakes and the driver to scream out the window, 'You tryin' to kill yourself? Who's in charge here?'

When Baron Ashura stepped into the headlights and waved his arms, the driver recognised him right away.

'What the hell?' the driver yelled. 'You trying to get my arse thrown in jail?'

'I warn them over and over, but they don't listen! Cut me some slack!'

'Do you know how many people've died out here under these trucks?'

'I'll take care of it!'

The Baron picked up a four-by-two and swung it about as he chased away the trash pickers who'd already climbed onto the pile. The pickers quickly backed off to behind the waiting line. Baron Ashura tried to catch his breath as he yelled, 'Who said you could go in without my signal? If there's an accident, we'll all get kicked out! You wanna blow your permit fees like that?'

After all of the trucks in his district had dumped their trash and left, the Baron raised one arm like a general leading his army and roared, 'Now!'

Forty-odd trash pickers ran toward the pile of garbage that towered over them. Though it was her first time, Bugeye's mother followed everyone else up the pile, scrambling on all fours, with Bugeye right on her tail. The Baron caught up with them and tossed a crumpled plastic bottle into her basket. While his mother picked through the better items in front, Bugeye followed behind and collected the second-line items that the Baron had told him to look out for: yogurt bottles, empty cosmetics jars, broken plastic dippers and basins, cans, glass bottles.

Most of the other trash pickers were wearing the types of headlamps that miners wore, and were able to spot higher-priced recyclables right away, but it was his mother's first day on the job, and not only was she unused to the work, it was still dark out. Even after turning something up with her pitchfork, she had to bring her face right up to it before she could see what it was. That was if she could grab it at all. The others closest to her didn't hesitate to snatch items away before she could get them. Bugeye stayed close to his mother, and grabbed whatever he could.

The work started at the top of the heap and made its way down: the pickers picked out items at random as they shuffled backwards, turning the trash over with their pitchforks as they went. By the time they made it to the bottom, the rubbish heap was flatter and more spread out than when they'd started. Back to the top they would go, digging their pitchforks in deeper and casting them about wider to pick out more items, and then they made their way over the top and down the other side to repeat the whole process, turning the mound of trash over bit by bit on their way down, and picking through it all again carefully on their way back up. It took them ten to fifteen minutes per truck, and when the first line was done, the second line came in to pick at the leftovers.

As day broke, the sky turned a deep red. The garbage was dirty and ugly, but it was also black and white and red and blue and yellow and iridescent and shiny, and it was smooth and square and angular and round and long and limp and stiff, and it refused to budge and it sprang out of the pile and it rolled down the slope, and it smelled acrid and it smelled foul, and it made your breath catch and your nose run and it made you gag, but above all, none of it looked familiar. When you looked at the trash one item at a time, the objects frightened you somehow, like seeing a leg that had fallen off a baby doll, even though you'd known all of these things forever. Bugeye foolishly sunk his pitchfork into something that had caused his mother to startle and shudder: a liquid something squirted out, and whatever it was got dragged up by the sharp prong of his pitchfork. The head looked like it belonged to a cat. The eyes were nothing but holes, and the sockets looked sunken, and he recognised it as a cat from the pointy ears on each side, but below the exposed fangs, the little belly was hollowed out. No, it wasn't hollow—it was packed with writhing maggots. The maggots spilled onto Bugeye's boots. He shuddered and threw it behind him. It was only later that he learned it, too, was just one of the many things the city discarded, no different from a crushed soda can or an empty soju bottle containing a cigarette butt with teeth marks still on it. Each item carried with it an air of sadness or regret, and maybe it was that air which left Bugeye feeling so frightened and out of place. When the sun rose, flies swarmed in and covered the bodies of the trash pickers and the piles of garbage.

The trucks never stopped rolling in, from every corner of the city. The landfill stretched along the river from the south-east to the south-west end of the island; the district sector was the length of seventy baseball fields, while the private sector was the length of a hundred-and-one fields. Twenty-one districts dumped their garbage there, but since the only people allowed to pick through the trash were those who had paid a permit fee through one of the crew leaders, each work crew was basically in charge of three or four different districts. When the first line finished one pile, they moved on to the next, and the second line would take the first line's place on the previous pile. Later, trucks carrying fill dirt would arrive and cover the garbage with earth, signalling an end to the morning's work.

2

A month had already passed since Bugeye and his mother moved to Flower Island. She had tried to console Bugeye at first by saying that people lived there just like anywhere else, but he knew it was a garbage dump filled with things used up and tossed aside, things people had grown tired of using, and things that were no longer of any use to anyone at all, and that the people who lived there were likewise discards and outcasts driven from the city.

Bugeye sometimes missed the crumbling streets of his old hillside slum. How wonderful it had been to wander uphill and downhill, getting lost in those steep, cramped alleyways that tunnelled off in all directions past cinder-block walls patched and mended with odds and ends, having his way blocked by shaggy, unwashed dogs humping in the middle of the alley, or by grannies sitting around in circles with their wrinkled, sagging breasts hanging halfway out of the bottoms of their torn, sleeveless undershirts as they got drunk on makkolli with each other right there in the street, picking his way through the scattered ash of spent coal briquettes and empty instant noodle wrappers skittering around in the wind, hearing a little girl sing from behind a tiny, opened window in the house that her parents locked before leaving for work, the baby on the girl's back almost as big as she was, and seeing the summer flowers dance in the wind beneath the flapping underwear hung out to dry behind the soy sauce and bean paste crocks, and the lamplit windows twinkling like stars against the darkened sky after nightfall, and the marketplace—the magnificent marketplace! The factory girls at the sweatshop where Bugeye did odd jobs used to crank up the radio and sing along or stuff fried *mandu* into Bugeye's mouth and laugh out loud, and the clothes they sewed were as beautiful as flowers. On the mat where his mother laid out her goods for sale at the market, the fresh, green vegetables were always damp with dew, and the fish in basins of water or on beds of ice were smooth and slick. There, everything was alive. But that didn't mean Bugeye hated Flower Island. It was simply a different world.

Although Bugeye had spent most of his time going back and forth between home and the marketplace along the alleyways of that hillside slum, he had been a part of the great city, and had access to buses and subway trains, buildings just on the other side of the overpass, schools, banks, police stations, movie theatres, all of it. But one day, Bugeye and his mother slipped, just like that, down a hole or into a well or perhaps through an old door, the way it happens in dreams, and found themselves transported to this strange and mysterious *dokkaebi* realm. Bugeye could not get over his amazement at how many different kinds of things were made and bought with money by all sorts of people, rich and poor, and then eaten or worn or used and thrown out, over and over and over again, all to end up in the same place.

Bugeye did as Baron Ashura had told him to do and joined his mother with the first line of trash pickers, not knowing any better at first, but an argument broke out among the grown-ups. The people in the second line complained to the Baron that he was playing favourites, and one woman even got right in Bugeye's mother's face and cursed at her. After that, Bugeye was demoted to the second line, where he was pushed around by the adults and had to pick through whatever was left and stack the items his mother flung from the pile and sort it all into categories.

Once every ten to fifteen days, scrap dealers came in hordes to purchase the items the pickers had salvaged and take it all to recycling plants. Though Baron Ashura's hauls did not contain the most profitable items, they weren't as pressed for choice as some of the others, but instead fell somewhere in between. The Baron's hauls came from the eastern and south-eastern districts, which were adjacent to the big marketplace downtown, as well as districts that included factories and rich folks' apartments. The private sectors controlled the commercial district in the heart of the city, the U.S. army base, the industrial complexes in the south-west corner of the city, and the sprawling upper-middle-class apartment complexes south of the river. Those sectors, with their privately owned trucks bearing names like Environmental Co-operative and Central Recycling, had exclusive contracts with each dump. They hired their own workers to collect recyclables, and would even purchase items from other trash pickers and resell them to recycling plants. Owners of private junkyards came and went as they pleased to carry off recyclables on the backs of their motorcycles, and peddlers showed up in small one-ton trucks to purchase items from the trash pickers, while the owners of private truck businesses came at regular intervals with huge Boxer or Titan trucks to haul everything away at once. On purchasing day, the trash pickers either sold their goods directly to the recycling plants or handed them off to the private truck companies if offered a good price.

On her first purchasing day, Bugeye's mother exclaimed that she'd made three times as much as she had working at the market, and went all the way down the hill to buy a crate of makkolli from the small shop there as a treat for the other pickers. Purchasing day was also when the adults who weren't working the night shift could go to a public bathhouse in the village across the stream and wash off the grime, get gussied up, and have a night out on the town.

Though it was partly the fault of the blue birthmark, Baron Ashura had rubbed Bugeye the wrong way from the start and earned his terrible nickname, and sure enough it seemed they were destined to be enemies. It was his mother's fault, really. Since the Baron had helped Bugeye and his mother to get settled and find work on Flower Island without having them pay a penny of their own money for the permit fee, Bugeye did as he was told, and though he could not bring himself to call the Baron 'Dad,' he might have been willing to call him 'Uncle.' But one night, Bugeye woke before dawn to find something amiss. He could tell that the thing next to him was not his mother. The thing pressed up and snoozing against his back was the size of a small child. Bugeye gave it a few pokes with his elbow. It mumbled something in its sleep and rolled over. What was Baldspot doing there? Ever since their first day on Flower Island, when Baldspot said that bullshit about the Baron sticking it in his mother, Bugeye had been determined to protect her. He nearly found himself channelling his father's voice and shouting, 'Goddamn son of a bitch, I'll kill them both!' Instead, he went outside and groped around in the dark for the kitchen knife that his mother kept in the box next to the entrance. He tugged on the door to the Baron's side of the shack (they called it a door, but it was really just a frame made from four-by-twos wrapped in plastic) but it was latched from the inside. Bugeye poked his finger right through the plastic, lifted the latch, and stepped inside. It was even darker there than it was outside. He regretted not having put on one of the headlamps they used for work. Just then, he heard a rustling sound, and something flashed before his eyes.

'Who's there?' hissed a low, threatening voice. 'Why, you little bastard ...'

Bugeye stepped back, holding up his arm to shield his eyes from the Baron's flashlight. The Baron, naked except for his underwear, lunged forward to grab him, but Bugeye managed to leap out the door. The Baron followed him outside and ran the flashlight beam over Bugeye.

'Well, look at that. Little shit's got a knife!'

'Who is it?'

When Bugeye heard his mother's voice coming from Baron Ashura's room, he dropped the knife and bolted down the path. He ran all the way up the hill until he reached the edge of the shantytown, and there he sat, gazing down at the river below, until the sun came up. Bugeye hadn't seen enough to know for sure what exactly the Baron and his mother were doing—maybe they'd only been hugging each other with their clothes off—but what he did know for sure was that the two of them would be sleeping under the same blanket from now on.

It took almost half an hour of staring off into space for his anger to subside; he even stopped feeling sore at his mother. Since he'd grown up by his wits, he more or less grasped how it was that grown-ups in a place like this lived. Kids here joked and laughed about their own and each other's parents like they were talking about perfect strangers. In any other place, that sort of talk would have led to fistfights and bloody noses, but the children of Flower Island merely snickered and tossed around some profanity. Many of the trash pickers had come there alone in search of work, and there were many mothers and fathers looking after their children on their own. There were, of course, unbroken families, but those folks mostly lived in the village across the stream, and commuted back and forth to Flower Island at dawn and dusk. The island was crammed with six thousand people living in two thousand households, the equivalent of scores of country villages put together. Naturally the adults were close with the other people in their work crews, but they also got to know pickers from neighbouring dumpsites, and spent many evenings drinking together. They fought hard, but made up harder, and men and women would get together and shack up for a few months before switching partners.

The children lived amongst themselves in a world separate from the adults. There were fewer than a dozen kids like Bugeye and Mole who had begun to put on grown-up airs and could pass back and forth between the adult world and the child world. There, by the time you were seventeen or eighteen, you had already fully crossed over. The scariest thing for kids like Bugeye and Mole were the older boys who'd just made the journey. In any case, among the many, many people living in that shantytown, Bugeye now found himself a reluctant member of a band of four. The family ties that Bugeye and his mother had been barely maintaining since his father went missing were severed that day.

When Bugeye saw the first line of garbage trucks start to make their way off the riverside expressway and cross the bridge onto the island, he stood and slowly made his way back down the hill. He didn't feel up to for reporting to work, and there wasn't much point in going back to the shack to sulk. He decided he would drop everything and play hooky instead. But he couldn't think of anywhere to go. Back in the city that he and his mother had been banished from, there was no end to the places where you could idle away the time: even aside from the hillside alleyways, there were playgrounds and parks and marketplaces and video arcades and comic-book stores.

Though the headquarters were not yet a place he could call his own, Bugeye decided to go there anyway and kill time until the noon shift. The last time he'd gone there, it was after dark and he was following Baldspot, so he thought it was close by and not too hard to find, but now the only thing he recognised was the river. Wasn't there a peanut patch …? He mumbled to himself as he stood and looked around, but the peanuts must have all been harvested—all he saw was dirt. Nevertheless he could tell from the dried-up leaves and stems littering the ground that something had grown there.

When he crossed the ridge on the other side of the field, he saw sand dunes, willow trees growing on the banks of the river, and a meadow overgrown with weeds and silver grass. Halfway up the slope, he found the low cinder-block wall that marked the hideout. He groped around in the sand for the hidden ropes and raised the awning, swept the sand from the linoleum, and sat there like he owned the place. Once inside, nothing of the outside world was visible; all he saw was the view afforded by the rectangular frame of the awning. To the left of the river, way off against the horizon, the sun was beginning to rise. The black of the river began to pale and gradually fade to white, and the glowing lights of apartment buildings far off across the river flickered on, one after the other, studding the darkness. Before long, it was bright enough to dampen the headlights of the cars driving up and down the expressway.

'*Hyung*!' Baldspot was standing in the centre of the frame, his cap cocked to one side. 'I knew you'd be here.'

Bugeye looked at Baldspot, who was all smiles, and said flatly, 'Hyung? Since when am I your older brother?'

'What did I tell you? I said my dad was going to stick it in your mum.'

Bugeye couldn't bring himself to get angry at Baldspot again, and just smiled weakly instead.

'So that's why you're calling me hyung now?'

'It's better than calling you Bugeye,' he giggled. 'Dad told me to come get you.'

Right about now, the adults would all be down on the hill of garbage digging mindlessly for gold. Bugeye wasn't mad anymore, despite himself, but he made up his mind to act like he was upset for a few more days and see how things panned out. There was no point in throwing a tantrum over his mother sleeping with another man, because the fact was that this land had no number and no address, and everyone and everything there was of no use to anyone. The only way a person could hope to get out of there was through some sort of recycling plant for people. The sun had risen completely, and the sunlight bouncing off the river's surface was like a billion tiny mirrors flashing at them. Baldspot and Bugeye sat and gazed out at the river.

Every day around this time, Bugeye got hungry, so if something to eat turned up as he was digging through the trash, he would sniff it first and then have himself a snack, whether it was yogurt or orange juice left over in the bottom of a carton, or a piece of fruit with a bite taken out of it, or an expired pastry still sealed in plastic.

The first shift of the day didn't end until around nine in the morning, after which everyone usually returned to their shacks to cook breakfast. The garbage trucks that had come from downtown and the city's commercial areas would leave for the day, and a fresh layer of fill dirt would be spread over the morning trash; the next round of trucks from apartment complexes and other residential areas would not arrive until afternoon.

The adults used the three hours in the morning after the first shift to sort through the items they'd collected and to take care of the day's cooking and cleaning. Some went to the shop at the bottom of the hill to buy things, and others got water from the water truck that came around twice a day. Still others went all the way down to the river to do laundry, or walked over to the village across the stream. After their late breakfast, they would be stuck at the dumpsite from around noon until sundown.

Late in the afternoon or in the evening, when they had finished sorting through the residential trash, the trucks from factories and industrial areas would come in. Along with the first shift, this was when they made the most money. Since this left the adults with little time to look after their families, the children were always hungry. Kids with parents were at least able to eat a combined breakfast and lunch, albeit a late one, when the adults had a little more time in the mornings, but in the evenings they had to use their wits to slip in amongst the grown-ups, who were usually busy getting drunk together in the empty lots between the rows of shacks after work ended, and grab whatever they could to eat. Some children would take the edible things that the adults had collected from the trash and get together in their homes or in any of the open fields on Flower Island to boil, grill, and steam their meals. Most of what they had to eat were canned foods or plastic packages of hot dogs past their expiration dates, or fish and other seafood that had been tossed out of the fish market, but neither the adults nor the children suffered much from stomach-aches or food poisoning. The runs were a problem, of course, but no one complained.

'Hungry?'

Bugeye pretended not to hear Baldspot's question. He didn't want to leave the hideout. Baldspot pulled out a wrinkled plastic package that crackled in his hands: inside were tightly packed rows of hot dogs. The side of the package was torn, and several of the hot dogs had already been eaten. Baldspot pulled one out and gave it a sniff; one side was covered in dirt.

'Smells good!' he said with a giggle.

Baldspot shoved the dirty hot dog into his mouth and sucked on it a few times, and then spat out the dirt and started to eat it. Back when he lived in the city, Bugeye thought, not only would he have never put something like that in his mouth, he would have beaten up the kid who offered it to him. But when he thought about it now, the hot dogs were probably chockfull of preservatives anyway and had obviously been sitting harmlessly in the corner of someone's fridge until they were eventually thrown out. Bugeye slipped one finger inside the plastic wrapper, pulled out a hot dog, and took a bite.

'Tastes good, too,' he said.

Baldspot and Bugeye had five each.

'There's something I've been wondering about,' Bugeye said. 'Last time you said you're the only one who sees the blue lights. What are they?'

Baldspot ducked down low and looked around to see if anyone could hear them.

'You're the only one I've told. None of the other kids can see them.'

'That's not what I asked.'

'I don't know what they are. They only come out at night. They look like us.'

'So, they're ghosts?'

'They're not scary. Some are kids; some are grown-ups. There are men and women, too.'

Baldspot's explanation made Bugeye lose interest. He didn't want to talk about those strange creatures anymore, so he changed the subject.

'How many kids use these headquarters?'

'Hmm, I think about six, including me. Only the kids who have the captain's permission are allowed here.'

Baldspot straightened his back with pride as he said this. Amused and annoyed at the same time, Bugeye muttered, 'So you're saying I shouldn't be here yet.'

'I don't know. Mole has to allow it.'

'This Mole, is he taller than me? Can he fight?'

'I think you're taller. But Mole is really strong.'

There were so many things Bugeye was curious about that he didn't stop there.

'What do you do all day?'

They lived right next to each other, and yet Bugeye only saw Baldspot in the late evenings. About a week after they'd moved to the island, Bugeye's mother had started making breakfast in Baron Ashura's kitchen, and they all ate together at the round metal-tray table. But Baldspot often didn't show up for meals, and Bugeye had been wondering where he went off to. In fact, he was gone so often that Bugeye's mother had begun to worry. Each time she asked the Baron where Baldspot was, the Baron either didn't respond or else he would frown, look over at Bugeye, and say, 'None of these little bastards here ever mind their parents.'

'No one goes to school?' Bugeye asked Baldspot.

'We have a school,' Baldspot said cheerily. 'I go when I feel like it. But today I feel like playing with you.'

'Do the other kids only go when they feel like it, too?'

'Yeah. There's a church down near the shop. That's where we go to school.'

'You're telling me that's where you spend all of your time?' Bugeye asked with a sneer of disbelief.

'No,' Baldspot said meekly. 'There's another place. I'm the only one who goes there. Scrawny's house.'

'Scrawny? Who's that?'

'You'll see. If you promise not to tell anyone, you can come too, hyung.'

Bugeye was bored with sitting in the hideout, just the two of them, doing nothing, so he got up and brushed the dirt off his pants. Like last time, Baldspot rushed ahead of him and led the way up the hill. When the little guy reached the top, he glanced back at Bugeye and headed down the other side of the hill, away from the shantytown. They were headed for the north-west corner of Flower Island. The backside of the hill was covered in silver grass and clover and foxtails, broken only by the occasional heap of scrap iron or discarded building materials. Bugeye could see a handful of farmers' huts and even a house made from cement blocks and a greenhouse made from vinyl sheeting down near the river.

As they made their way between cabbage patches, Bugeye heard a dog start to yap loudly from inside the cement-block house, followed by a staccato chorus as more dogs joined in, barking and yapping. The door of the boxy little house opened, and a woman with her hair sticking up in all directions leaned out.

'Little Uncle's here!' she said.

She looked like she was about thirty. She wore a bright-blue hiking shirt and baggy pants covered in an oversize floral pattern, and her short hair had been tightly permed at one point but was since losing its curl and now bristled out like a comic book character getting electrocuted.

Cradled in one arm was a scrawny dog no bigger than a fist. The little creature was barking wildly and baring its teeth. Its bark was so shrill and sharp that Bugeye worried its vocal chords might snap. As if that wasn't enough, ten more small dogs inside the house began barking, too, each trying to outdo each other.

'Come in, come in! They'll calm down as soon as I close the door.'

Bugeye followed Baldspot into the house and watched as Baldspot petted each of the dogs in turn. To his surprise, when Baldspot brought his hand up to the mouth of the little dog that the woman held in her arm, the little creature licked Baldspot's palm. The house soon grew quiet.

'Sit, sit,' the woman said and then asked, 'Who's your friend?'

'He's my hyung,' Baldspot said.

'I didn't know you had an older brother.'

'He fell off a garbage truck!' he said with a giggle.

'Well now, what can't you get from a garbage truck these days?' the woman chuckled.

The look on her face said she had no further questions about Bugeye's surprise visit. Baldspot took the little dog from her and sat it on his lap. In an attempt to be courteous to their host, Bugeye reached out to pet the dog, but the little thing gave a loud yap and bit the back of his hand. It was so unexpected and painful that Bugeye yelled and jumped right out of his seat. The other dogs bristled or hid their tails and backed away from him, barking wildly.

'Scrawny! Hush!'

Baldspot gave the dog a shake. The dog wagged its tail and stuck its head in Baldspot's lap. If that had happened away from the house, Bugeye thought to himself, he'd have given that dog a swift kick or dropped it on the ground. But, to his wonder, as soon as Scrawny stopped yapping, the other dogs quieted as well.

'Scrawny's the captain of this house,' Baldspot said with a giggle, as he scratched the dog's stomach.

'She's the oldest and was the first to come live with us,' the woman explained.

The little dog seemed to know they were talking about her, because she gazed up, weepy-eyed, at the woman. Now Bugeye understood why Baldspot had called this place Scrawny's house. He also learned that all of the dogs were elderly, over sixty in people years, and that not one of them was in good shape. Scrawny was a purebred Chihuahua, around thirteen years old, while the other dogs were mutts of varying breeds. There were dogs with long matted hair, dogs with short hair, dogs with curly hair; grey dogs, black dogs, brown dogs; dogs with brindled coats, dogs with spotted coats; dogs with long legs, dogs with short legs; dogs with long snouts, dogs with stubby snouts; dogs of every shape and misshape; dogs with crippled back legs, dogs with crippled front legs; dogs with two broken legs, dogs with bow legs; dogs with one torn ear, dogs missing one eye.

'Little Uncle got here just in time. I was about to feed the dogs.'

The woman pulled a motley collection of bowls from the cupboard: the lid from a clay jar, an earthenware bowl, a dented washbasin made of nickel, a porcelain dish, a plastic saucer from underneath a flower pot. She lined up the dogs' food bowls on the linoleum floor between the two bedrooms in the narrow space that served as both kitchen and living room. When Baldspot dragged out the bag of dog food and began scooping the food into the bowls, the dogs rushed over. Scrawny was served her own special meal of a handful of rice mixed with tuna in a stainless-steel doggy bowl. But she walked away after just a few bites. Baldspot explained why Scrawny's meal was different.

'She's a sick old granny. We have to encourage her to eat.'

While the dogs ate, the only sound was of chewing and bowls rattling. Just then, more barking was heard out in the yard. The woman looked out the window.

'Time to feed the rest.'

Bugeye peeked outside. There were more dogs in the greenhouse.

The woman looked at Baldspot and said, 'I saw the *dokkaebi* lights last night, the whole Mr. Kim family, way off in the distance.'

'I saw them, too, a few days ago, down by the bend in

the stream. Mr. Kim didn't talk to me.'

'Still, if they showed themselves to you, that must mean they like you.'

The dogs emptied their bowls and walked around, peeking into each other's bowls, and either sprawling out flat or growling at each other. They weren't as playful as regular dogs. Some dragged their hind legs behind them; others hopped around on three legs. When another dog came over to her bowl and lapped up the rest of her food, Scrawny cowered and crawled onto Baldspot's lap again. The tiny dog let out a long sigh, sounding very much like a little old lady, and gazed up at Bugeye through watery eyes.

'Where did all of these dogs come from?' Bugeye asked, addressing the woman for the first time since he'd gotten there.

Instead of answering, Baldspot and the woman looked at each other and smiled. Bugeye was well aware that no one would have actually paid money for these filthy, mangy creatures.

'Peddler Grandpa collects everything,' Baldspot giggled.

'These dogs were thrown out by people,' the woman explained. 'Like everything else here.'

She told him that they'd started with just one or two dogs that had either gotten lost or were abandoned, but as more and more older neighbourhoods in the city were torn down and replaced with new apartment buildings, the number of abandoned dogs had increased as well, and so here she was. Baldspot headed out to the yard to feed the rest of the dogs, with Bugeye following right behind him. The woman lifted the lid on a large cooking pot, fashioned from a discarded oil drum, sitting on top of a brazier. She peeked inside.

'Lots of vittles today!' she exclaimed.

The woman's father, Peddler Grandpa, collected leftover food every few days from restaurants in the city. The woman used scraps of paper and cardboard to stoke the fire beneath the cooking pot. At the sound of people shuffling around in the yard, the dogs got worked up all over again and began to bark louder. When Baldspot opened the door to the greenhouse, they barked and whined and whipped their tails back and forth as they crowded around him. Even Bugeye had three or four dogs jump at him and rest their paws on him or leap high to lick at his hands. The thirty or so dogs in the greenhouse were as varied in size and appearance as the ailing, elderly dogs inside the house, and there were quite a few big dogs among them as well. The woman added dog food to the leftovers boiling in the pot, then ladled it into plastic bowls, while Baldspot and Bugeye ferried the bowls into the greenhouse and set them down in one long row. Afterward, they went back inside and ate *sujebi* soup that the woman had prepared for their own lunch.

Baldspot and Bugeye spent the rest of the day playing and hanging out near Scrawny's house. The junk that

Peddler Grandpa brought home was sorted into neat piles outside. Refrigerators and washing machines kept to their own circles, while televisions and computers were stacked on top of each other like brick buildings. Glass shards and sheet-metal were spread out in the work yard where electronics were disassembled. Glass bottles that had once held beer, soju, cola, or other beverages sat in a crate; cardboard boxes that had been taken apart were tied together in bundles; tiny plastic items were gathered inside buckets and baskets; and large items of similar size were roped together.

Peddler Grandpa arrived late in the afternoon behind the wheel of his one-ton truck. More junk, strapped down with bungee cords, filled the back of the truck, towering well overhead. Peddler Grandpa was a short, balding man in his sixties with a white beard. Like the other junkyard owners and private truck drivers, he purchased discarded items and resold them to recycling plants, and collected electronics from different parts of the city and took them apart himself to sell the components. The work of dismantling electronics took place once every few days with the help of the occasional women or elderly men who lived nearby and found themselves with a little free time in the afternoon.

That day, Bugeye came to have a newfound respect for Baldspot. In the shantytown where they lived, children were useless, worth less than scrap metal. To make matters worse, no one wanted to deal with a kid like Baldspot, who was slow and stammered when he spoke. For the grown-ups, who had to work nonstop from dawn to dusk, children were nothing more than an obstacle that slowed them down. Bugeye suspected that Baldspot merely pretended to be simpleminded but was actually clever and given to deep thoughts. The hideout had only impressed him a little—every neighbourhood had a place like that where kids could play, after all—but the sights he saw at Scrawny's house were enough to knock him down a peg.

The greenhouse and Peddler Grandpa's junkyard were not the only surprises to be found behind Scrawny's house. From the back of the house all the way out to the western-most corner of triangular Flower Island stood a forest of trees and plants, both big and small: from willows, elms, and mulberries, to bush clover and wild roses. Along the river's edge, silver grass, cattails, and reeds rose up over Bugeye's head. When Baldspot suggested going down later to the bend in the stream on the other side of the forest, Bugeye felt bothered by the way the little guy lowered his voice and shifted his eyes around. It made him uneasy to have spent the whole afternoon loafing around at a stranger's house.

'Let's go home. They're probably looking for us.'

'We'll be fine until sunset,' Baldspot said. 'Unless you really want to leave now.'

Baldspot went in to say goodbye, giving Bugeye no

choice but to follow him. But when they stepped inside, they heard quiet music start to play somewhere in the house. The woman's shoulders began to rise and fall, her arms crisscrossed her chest, and her whole body shook. As Baldspot hurriedly searched around, the woman turned her head and gestured with her chin.

'It's in there,' she said through gritted teeth.

Bugeye recognised the melody. *Hey, you silly sleepyhead, sun is up, why are you still in bed, time to get up, ding dong dang, ding dong dang!* The woman's legs went stiff, and she fell flat on her back. Her arms stretched out to the sides, her legs twisted and flailed. Her eyes rolled back until only the whites were showing, and her mouth foamed like a crab's. Baldspot ran into the room and turned off the alarm clock, but the woman was still writhing on the floor, her limbs stiff. Bugeye was so frightened that he ran for the door and grabbed his shoes, ready to make his escape.

'What's wrong with her?' he yelled.

Baldspot calmly folded a thin floor cushion in half, placed it under the woman's head, and kept watch over her.

'It's time,' he said with his characteristic giggle.

Not only was Baldspot not surprised by any of it, he just sat there, completely unperturbed and smiling away at Bugeye as though he was used to this sort of thing. After a while, the woman sat back up, dishevelled, and stared as if she were seeing the two of them for the first time.

'You're early today,' Baldspot said.

Bugeye had no idea what was going on, and kept looking back and forth between the two of them. The woman finally seemed to recognise Baldspot, and turned her gaze instead to Bugeye.

'You're the dogs' uncle,' she said to Baldspot, 'but who's that kid?'

'My hyung. He fell off a garbage truck. Who am I talking to?'

'Granny Willow, from down by the water.'

'Aren't you kind of young to be a granny?'

'I used to be a young bride, but now I'm old so I'm a granny.'

'Why have you come to visit us?'

'I'm this woman's guardian spirit. She worries too much, and asked for my help.'

Baldspot spoke nonchalantly with the woman, whose voice and facial expressions had changed completely. The woman pulled up the hood of her hiking shirt and headed out the door. Baldspot and Bugeye followed. Peddler Grandpa, who had been outside in the yard sorting through the items he'd collected, seemed to understand at once what was happening, because he pulled off his cotton gloves and headed over. He reached out his hand to stroke his daughter's cheek and pry back her eyelids.

'You were fine for so long, but now you're out of your mind again?'

The woman made no move to brush his hand away,

and only said in a docile-sounding voice, 'I'll cook dinner after I'm back from the village.'

'Stay home. Play with the kids and the dogs.'

She pretended not to hear him, and strode off into the trees with her arms swinging. As Baldspot and Bugeye moved to follow her, Peddler Grandpa warned them, 'Don't let her go far. Bring her home before it gets dark.'

They made their way through the thickening underbrush until they reached a spot where the silver grass grew up over their heads. Bugeye stopped. The woman forged ahead, parting the grass with her hands. Baldspot stayed right on her heels.

'Where's she going?' Bugeye called out.

Baldspot looked back at him and said, 'The bend in the stream. Not just anyone can go there.'

Bugeye didn't want to go further, but he followed them anyway, using both hands to push through the tall grass that scratched his face and whipped him in the eyes. The trees began to get taller, and patches of sand appeared in their shade. In a circle of trees stood a small shrine, half-collapsed. The door was missing and the roof tiles had fallen off, exposing the mixture of clay and sorghum straw underneath. An old tree standing next to the shrine was wider around than arms could reach, but it didn't look all that tall. Fresh, green leaves still sprouted from the long, slender branches that grew out in all directions from the trunk, which was pocked with holes from where the wood had rotted. Later, Peddler Grandpa would explain to Bugeye that the shrine was the original guardian shrine for Flower Island, and the old willow that had grown there for hundreds of years was its sacred tree. Long ago, the residents of the island had held shamanic rituals there, but as their village was gone now, the shrine had naturally fallen into disrepair. What Bugeye learned right away was that, aside from the hideout, the bend in the stream was the most wonderful place to be at sundown. The top of the hillock at the western-most edge of the island offered up the best view of river and sky lit with the glow of the setting sun. The woman rubbed her hands together in prayer as she circled the shrine, picking up scraps of old wooden boards as she went, and trying to fit them back together neatly.

'*Aigo*, families should stay together. Not scatter themselves about so.'

The woman, or Scrawny's mama, as Bugeye would come to know her, kept muttering under her breath and wandering in circles. She picked up a tree branch that had fallen next to a rock, caressed it gently over and over, and then tossed it back into the grass.

'Man of the house has got to have some backbone,' she mumbled, 'if the rest of the family is to have any strength.'

Baldspot followed right behind her, smiling and giggling, while Bugeye kept his distance. He carefully examined the wooden ledge that ran around the sides of the collapsed shrine; the vines that crawled over the rocks, stone steps, and scattered roof tiles; the spiderwort and plantain and wormwood and even goosefoot that grew thick and verdant in the sandy earth.

Suddenly the woman turned her back on the setting sun and became a black shadow that asked Baldspot, 'Do you know who I am?'

'Granny Willow, of course!' he answered with his usual giggle.

Undaunted, Bugeye warned Baldspot, 'We were told to get her home before dark.'

Bugeye thought it plainly obvious that Scrawny's mama was a crazy woman half out of her mind, but he didn't dare say it out loud. Bugeye and Baldspot each took her by a hand and walked her home. When they made it back to the junkyard, the woman's father was waiting out front. He put his arm around her shoulders and led her inside. The dogs leaped and barked with joy. The sun was setting, and the sky was growing dark.

'Looks like we'll have to call in a shaman and hold a ceremony for her,' Peddler Grandpa muttered.

'She's not sick,' Baldspot said.

'I'm worried she'll take off and wander around again like she did last time. I have to work. I can't stay here all day with her. The two of you should come by as often as you can.'

At some point, the woman seemed to return to her

senses. She slowly got up and began preparing dinner, while the boys headed out into the lowering dusk. Bugeye realised that he was now Baldspot's closest friend. Though there would be others who knew about the hideout, he was the only one who knew about Scrawny's house.

The two of them crossed the fallow fields and the ploughed furrows of the farmers who lived in the village across the stream, which had not yet been taken over by landfill, as they made their way east toward the shantytown.

'You can't tell anyone we came here,' Baldspot said in a voice heavy with maturity.

'I won't tell a soul,' Bugeye said obediently, without a trace of scorn. 'I'll keep it secret.'

A great many things were still confusing to Bugeye, but since he could not be blunt with Baldspot, he tried to ask indirectly about some of them.

'Those creatures that you said looked like blue lights before, were those *dokkaebi*?'

'Shh!' Baldspot glanced around at the darkening field and lowered his voice. 'They might be nearby.'

'Was Scrawny's mama possessed by the spirit of a willow tree just now?'

'Duh.'

Bugeye couldn't bring himself to say what he wanted to say, which was, *You're all nuts*. But if nothing else, this day had been the most fun he'd had since moving to Flower Island. The secret he had come to share with

Baldspot made him feel reassured somehow. His stupid mother could sponge off the Baron all she wanted, now he had a new world of his own to enjoy.

They were just passing the dug-up peanut patch when someone suddenly popped out of the darkness.

'Oy, Baldspot!'

Startled, Baldspot tried to run away, but two more boys came after him and wrestled him to the ground. Bugeye stood facing the biggest of the three kids, who blocked his path, and debated in his mind whether or not to intervene. Though the kid was big, he was only a bit bigger than the other two, and looked like he was about a head shorter than Bugeye.

'You the new guy?'

Bugeye figured this must be Mole. He'd already heard all about him from Baldspot, and knew that he could not be the first to back down.

'Nice to meet you. I'm Bugeye.'

The two boys on the ground giggled at his nickname, but Mole frowned and said, 'How old're you?'

'Fifteen.'

Bugeye added two years to his age, just as he used to do back in his old neighbourhood whenever he was confronted by older kids. Still pinned to the ground, Baldspot yelled,

'He works for my dad!'

Mole visibly relaxed.

'Whatever. I was here first, which makes me your

hyung. I hear you two've been hanging out at headquarters without my permission.'

Bugeye understood now why the boys had jumped him and Baldspot as soon as they saw them. One of the boys must have spotted the two of them either going to or coming back from the hideout. Bugeye figured there was no reason for him to make an enemy of Mole, so he smiled.

'Baldspot was telling me about you,' he said. 'We went to see if you were there.'

'What for?'

'So we could be friends, what else?'

Bugeye held his hand out the way adults did when they wanted to shake hands. Mole turned his head and scoffed.

'Look at this guy, trying to get on my good side,' Mole said, but he took Bugeye's hand lightly and just as quickly let go.

As soon as they'd shaken hands, the mood changed completely. Mole led the way up the hill to the hideout, and everyone else followed behind. When they got to the hideout, they raised the awning, and Mole lit a couple of candles. He set the plastic bags on top of the table and squatted down.

'Hey, the ground is all dewy. My bum's wet. We better build a roof.'

Bugeye surmised that Mole had been planning to make dinner out there with the others. Mole pulled ingredients out of the bags. The boys all got to work without having to be told what to do, toting the food and cans down to the river's edge, while Baldspot prepared some kindling by tearing up a cardboard box and placing the pieces inside a stove that had been fashioned from part of an oil can. Mole looked over at where Bugeye was sitting off to one side by himself.

'You said your name is Bugeye? Think you could build us a roof for next time?'

'Yeah, sure, a roof'd be good. If you help me, I could build one by tomorrow or the next day.'

'I work in one of the private sectors, man. I'm busy. But I'll tell you what. I'll pull together some lumber or whatever else you need so you and Baldspot can make us something nice.'

The boys finished prepping the ingredients and came back from the river. They'd filled empty cans with water, and cleaned and gutted two fish that had come out of the trash from the fish market. Bugeye had seen a lot of this sort of thing since arriving on the island: even food that was on the verge of spoiling or was well past its expiration date tasted delicious once it had been boiled with some hot pepper paste or fermented soybean paste. Then, if you threw in some instant ramen noodles or a hunk of cold rice, it was worth fighting over. Hidden under the low table in the hideout were pots and empty cans, and even spoons and disposable chopsticks. Baldspot lay on his stomach in front of the small, soot-blackened stove, and added strips of corrugated cardboard to get the fire started. All at once, the air filled with the smell of burning plastic. Mole smacked Baldspot on the back of the head.

'Dumbarse! Now it stinks! I told you to scrape the stove out clean before you light the fire.'

'Still smells better than where we live,' Bugeye said.

Mole took the comment in his stride.

'That's why we built these headquarters,' he said.

It made sense. If Baldspot had not shown him the hideout when he first came to the island with his mother, Bugeye might have felt so hopeless that he would've tried to run away at once. Baldspot gave up on stoking the fire, and backed away from the stove with a pout. He looked upset about getting hit on the head.

The boys cooked their dinner away from the swarms of flies crowding the garbage, away from the grown-ups, down by the river's edge where the air was heady with the scent of grass and flowing water. Afterward, they lay side by side on a big scrap of canvas. Mole first, of course. The glow of the streetlights from the riverside highway and the lights of the city across the river turned the sky milky, but a few stars still managed to flicker their way through. Mole pulled out a cigarette that he'd found who-knows-where, and lit it. He took a few puffs and held it over Bugeye's face.

'Take a puff.'

Bugeye hesitated before taking the cigarette. Older boys had tried before to get him to smoke. He'd refused and had to put up with endless teasing about how he was still just a kid and how if he didn't smoke he would never manage to grow any hair around his dick, and so this time he went ahead and, acting as if he knew what he was doing, took a puff and coolly exhaled. He knew that if he so much as coughed the tiniest bit, he would be dismissed as an amateur, so he blew a big, long gush of smoke into the air. Luckily, Mole was staring at the sky and didn't notice how awkward Bugeye was at it. Bugeye took a few more puffs and raised his hand to offer it to the next person. The boy lying next to him, the one they called Toad, snatched it away.

'It'll be Chuseok in a few days,' Mole muttered.

Surprised, Bugeye asked, 'Do people celebrate holidays here, too?'

'Yeah, some people even do the memorial service. The grown-ups'll all go party.'

'Where?'

'Across the river, in the city. That place has everything.'

Mole turned to look at Bugeye and added, 'I'm losing face by being friends with you, but whatever. This place is nothing but little kids who spend all their time at the church school. Not like I've got anyone better to hang out with. Just build me a roof in exchange.'

'Yeah, sure. But hey, that means I can call you Mole instead of hyung now, right?'

'Fucking hell, maybe I should get a new nickname.'

To his relief, Bugeye's admission into the hideout was not the hazing that Baldspot had worried it would be.

3

As always, the sorting of garbage from the downtown and commercial areas began at dawn and ended around nine in the morning. Bulldozers levelled out the heaps of trash, then dump trucks loaded with fill dirt came in to cover the trash. The pickers on the Baron's team gathered the items they'd scavenged into baskets and carried them over to the clearing that served as the sorting area. Up and down between the dumpsite and the sorting area they went, collecting the results of their morning's work, separating it into different categories, weighing everything, and confirming the amounts. The crew leaders wrote down how much everyone collected each day. Then, twice a month, on purchasing day, all of the items they'd collected were sold in bulk to recycling plants, and the money was divvied up according to each person's individual haul.

Since it was the day before the Chuseok holiday, the trash from the commercial areas had multiplied over the last few days, and far more food waste had been spilling out of the trucks that came from the apartment complexes and residential areas in the afternoon. But it was clear that the real flood of trash wouldn't hit them until two or three days after Chuseok. Here, as in the city, this time of year was referred to as the Chuseok rush. The whole country would be on holiday for the three-day-long autumn harvest celebration, after which the landfill would be deluged with paper and plastic and cardboard of all sorts. The pickers were already worried about whether they'd get a moment's break at all the next week.

'Go fetch some water,' Bugeye's mother said as soon as they got to the hut.

Bugeye grabbed two white plastic water jugs from the kitchen of Baron Ashura's hut, which was now their home, too, and headed down to the water truck. This time of day—when Bugeye and his mother, Baldspot and the Baron, all sat around late in the morning eating breakfast face to face—wasn't exactly intolerable to him, but he was finding it more and more uncomfortable as time went on. The Baron had naturally become head of the family, and his mother had obediently become his woman. He was strict in his rule that the family should always eat breakfast together, so Bugeye and Baldspot ate their meals at the tiny metal tray table, their heads nearly touching.

Baldspot sometimes went to the church school and sometimes didn't, and yet the Baron was indifferent as to whether or not the kid actually ever studied. Baldspot wasn't allowed to work like Bugeye, digging items out of the trash heaps directly, but he did his best to help out by standing in the back and putting the items that the others had picked into baskets or carrying the baskets for them. On the days that Baldspot announced he was going to school, no one stopped him or pressured him to work instead. In fact, not even Bugeye worked all three shifts like his mum did, from dawn to afternoon and on into the night. Though he never missed the morning shift, with its delivery of trash from the downtown and commercial areas, he sometimes skipped the afternoon sorting of residential trash or the nightfall sorting of trash from factories and construction sites. On Mondays, when there was more work, the Baron would order him to help his mother, but the rest of the time Bugeye could excuse himself by saying he was going to school with Baldspot, and the Baron refrained from scolding him.

This time of the day, the little shop and the water truck were always crowded with women and children getting ready to cook. Bugeye set his water jugs at the back of a long, motley line of containers, and waited politely off to the side with the others. Past the shop and the management office were a half-moon-shaped Quonset hut that had been built recently and two khaki-coloured army tents that served as the church. Some sort of event seemed to be going on: a colourful banner had been hung, and cars and vans were parked out front, the sunlight glaring off the vehicles. Hymns blared out of a bugle-shaped loudspeaker on the roof of the Quonset hut. Bugeye got his turn at the water truck and filled both jugs. He picked one up in each hand and started to walk, but they were impossibly heavy. He staggered along a ways, stopped to catch his breath, staggered some more. He was just passing the crowded shop when he spotted Baldspot's baseball cap.

'Hey! Baldspot!'

Baldspot turned at the sound of Bugeye's voice and ran over, looking glad to see him.

'Hyung! Did you come to get water?'

'What, you can't tell by looking? Where've you been all morning? You skipped breakfast.'

'I'm going to the church school. They're handing out ramen noodles and rice cake.'

'Really? Can I go, too?'

'Any kid from here can go.'

'Great. Help me with these water jugs, and I'll join you.'

Baldspot and Bugeye slowly made their way along the path to the shantytown, shifting the jugs from left to right as they went. Bugeye made it home much faster with Baldspot's help. His mother carried the jugs into their shack.

'Look at that, I've got two helpers today,' she said.

When she saw that they were about to take off again without coming inside, she asked, 'Don't you need to eat breakfast? Your father'll be angry at you.'

'Baldspot said we'll get ramen and rice cake if we go to

church today,' Bugeye said.

His mother's face lit up slightly, and she said, 'Ramen, huh? Better get a move on then. And bring some back with you.'

Bugeye and Baldspot darted off down the narrow path, speed-walked past the front of the shop, and headed over to the church. The hymn had already been replaced by the sound of the preacher clamouring out a prayer through the loudspeaker.

'That's the worship service,' Baldspot said. 'They don't give us stuff until that's over.'

Baldspot knew exactly what to do. Bugeye followed him into the army tent that was used as a classroom. Bugeye had once come looking for Baldspot here, so he knew that one tent was for the kindergarteners and the other was for the grade schoolers. The kindergarten tent had a worktable, vinyl flooring, and wooden shelves filled with cheap plastic toys, and the grade-school tent had desks and chairs and even a chalkboard that could be wheeled around—all of which had been salvaged from the trash. Bugeye and Baldspot's target was the kindergarten tent. Cardboard boxes and Styrofoam food containers were stacked inside, and a man and a woman were hanging a banner that read in large letters 'Heaven's Church Mission' against the back wall. Baldspot and Bugeye decided to wait outside the tent.

When the service ended, the door to the Quonset hut opened, and people poured out. The first to emerge were the children and the volunteers who taught night school, then a grey-haired pastor in a suit and a preacher in bedraggled coveralls walking next to him, followed by a gaggle of women who looked nothing like the folks who lived in the landfill. These outside visitors, first of all, had milky-pale skin and wore makeup, and some of the women wore fancy dresses with cardigans over their shoulders or trench coats and hats, while other women wore suits. Some had brought their children. There were about thirty or so visitors in all.

'Okay, everyone, let's take a photo,' a young woman with a camera called out. 'This way, please.'

The pastor, the church elder, the head of the women's ministry, the preacher, and everyone else lined up automatically beneath the banner without having to be told where to stand. Most of the visitors were middle-aged women, and as they lined up in two rows, the dreary interior of the army tent suddenly brightened. Even the children stood politely next to their mothers. When they were all grouped together, the air around them smelled like a flower garden.

The woman with the camera hanging from her neck called out, 'You kids, come over here and sit in front.'

The children who'd been standing outside the tent all rushed in, but the preacher raised his arms to stop them.

'Grade schoolers, stay where you are. Let's have just the kindergarteners.'

The bigger kids slunk back outside, including Bugeye and Baldspot, while the kindergarteners lined up and sat at the adults' feet, as instructed by the female volunteers. When the head of the women's ministry jumped out of line and grabbed the youngest child—a three-year-old—and squatted down with her on her lap, the rest of the women scrambled to follow suit and pose with a small child on their laps or in their arms. From the front, the kindergarteners and the adults lined up behind them were so drastically different in both attire and appearance that it looked like a scene from a documentary about travellers in the wilds of some remote jungle.

As Bugeye stood outside and watched them take the photo, he felt a sudden jolt, like he'd been punched in the chest. One face inside the tent began to glow brighter and brighter, while everyone else's faded into the background. The girl's hair hung straight down past her cheeks and just brushed her shoulders, not too long and not too short, and her face was slender and fair. Her lips glistened. Her school uniform was a dark chocolate brown, and the woman next to her, who appeared to be her mother, had one arm wrapped around her. She had to be the same age as Bugeye, maybe just a year or two older. Girls like her all seemed to have the same air about them.

Just down the hill and across a pedestrian overpass from the hillside slum where Bugeye had once lived was an entirely different world. There were middle-class homes, each with their own similarly sized yards planted with flowers and trees, and as you walked further into the neighbourhood, there was a hillside, still with its original forest, which served as the area's sole park. At the base of the hill were expensive houses surrounded by big yards, and at every corner of the well-maintained roads was a neighbourhood patrol-guard post.

Bugeye first saw the girl while crossing the pedestrian overpass. He was on his way home from the market a few bus stops away; she was probably on her way home from school. Judging by her uniform, she must've been in middle school. People streamed past to the left and right of him, but the moment he saw her in the distance, he felt like it was just the two of them, walking towards each other. And that was where his memory stopped. Afterwards he took to loitering around the overpass, making his way up and down, trying to judge the time. At last, another opportunity arrived for him to come face to face with her. He saw the girl get off a bus and head up the stairs, so he went up the stairs on the other side. This time, there were hardly any other pedestrians. A man dressed in a suit and tie and carrying a briefcase came towards him fast, and trailing behind was the girl, walking at her usual slow, steady pace. He studied the tiny birthmark above her cheek and the slender pin that held back her bangs. She glanced at him once, as if he were of no more interest than a street sign or the railing of the overpass, and walked on by. Bugeye couldn't bear to watch her walk away, so he kept going until he got to the end of the overpass before turning to look. She had just reached the bottom of the stairs and had set one foot on the footpath. He started to walk towards her and then stopped. What was his old name again, he wondered, back when he, too, was an ordinary boy who went to school like the other kids? Jeong-ho? That was it. Choi Jeong-ho. He murmured his real name to himself as he slowly headed back to the hillside slum.

He didn't see her again until much, much later. It might have been around when the seasons were changing. He remembered wearing a heavy, corduroy jacket, which meant it had to have been winter. Bugeye was hanging out by the overpass around the same time as usual when he spotted the girl again. This time, instead of crossing the bridge, he waited for her to come down the stairs, and followed her at a distance. The girl walked to a residential area near the far end of the park, past one of the guard posts, and disappeared behind an iron gate at the top of a staircase. Bugeye was standing at the bottom of a very high wall, gazing up at the top of it, when a middle-aged man dressed in a dark-blue security guard uniform ambled up to him and, with no warning, grabbed Bugeye by the scruff of his neck.

'What're you doing here?'

'Nothing,' Bugeye exclaimed.

'Where do you live, kid?'

'Across the bridge.'

The security guard looked Bugeye up and down. 'Quit hanging around here,' the guard said, 'and get yer arse back home.'

Bugeye thought about his father then. Were these the same kind of iron gates his father had gone around stealing?

After the group photo, another photo was taken to commemorate the donation of five hundred boxes of instant ramen noodles—care packages provided by the women's ministry from Heaven's Church. The head of the women's ministry and the preacher held up a box together and smiled for the camera. Many of the visitors had cameras of their own, and they took photo after photo of each other. Yet even while snapping pictures, the women kept looking around warily and covering their noses with both hands. One young woman who'd been taking photos was spraying air freshener, as if to chase the smell away. Those who lived there smelled it all the time and so had stopped noticing it, but the grown-ups said that whenever they went to the marketplace in town, other people would look around and pinch their noses as they passed. Changing their clothes made no difference.

The tent church on Flower Island tended to have a lot of these events, as there were frequent visits from churchgoers who lived in the apartment complexes and residential areas of the city. Many came in person, but at holidays, items poured in from all directions. People from community organisations, bureaucrats from city hall, and even National Assembly members came by bearing gifts. There were events held just for the grown-ups living on Flower Island, but most of the church events were targetted at children and the trash pickers who attended church services.

At last, the visitors started handing out the food. The children stood in two lines, one for kindergarteners and the other for grade schoolers. The kindergarten line was mostly mothers and their children; kindergarteners who'd come alone were asked for their information and told the food would be delivered directly to their shacks. Bugeye and Baldspot got in the middle of the grade-school line. Bugeye didn't notice until after they cut in that the girl and her mother were standing side by side at the head of the grade-schoolers' line. The mother was handing out boxes of ramen, while the girl handed out the styrofoam food containers. He knew it was not the same girl he'd dared to follow all the way to her house in the woods, but it was the first time since that day that his heart had raced this fast and that he found it so impossible to stand still, just as if he were fighting the urge to pee. He wanted to get out of line and run away, but they were already well inside the tent, and his turn was almost there. He had no choice but to follow on the heels of the kid in front of him and approach the table.

The girl and her mother were giving everyone one box of ramen and one styrofoam container each. No one in line pushed or shoved. They could see for themselves from the towering stacks of boxes behind the table that there was no fear of running out before they'd had their turn. Baldspot took his rations first, and then it was Bugeye's turn. Right before his eyes was the necklace hanging from the throat of the mother in her two-piece suit and just below that the girl's fair face. The mother handed him a box of ramen, and the daughter handed him a styrofoam food container. The girl smiled right at him, and Bugeye felt all of the strength drain out of his legs and threaten to dump him onto the ground. Just then, the preacher, who'd been standing behind the two women, spoke up.

'I've never seen you before.'

'I just moved here.'

'Hm. Make sure you come to church next time.'

Bugeye found himself automatically saying, 'Yes sir,' in a barely audible voice before turning to go, his face burning bright red. As soon as he was outside, Baldspot poked his face out from the crowd of children and said, 'Almost didn't get food, did ya?'

'Ugh, that was embarrassing ...'

Bugeye ran ahead, worried that one of the church people might try to stop him. Children who'd come out of the tents were already pulling the rubber bands from around the styrofoam containers and eating the half-moon-shaped *songpyeon* rice cakes. The rich scent of sesame oil filled the air. Bugeye and Baldspot were passing the front of the shop, their boxes of ramen tucked under their arms, when they saw a crowd of women rushing towards the church with their children in tow. News of the food must have spread. One of the women stopped Bugeye. Her eyes were fixed on the box of ramen clasped tightly to his side.

'Did they run out?'

Baldspot spread his arms wide, and said with that giggle of his, 'There's still *this* much left.'

Bugeye was overcome with shame, not only at himself but at all of the women stampeding towards the church and everyone else he lived with on that island. *What a fucking joke*, he thought.

At the entrance to the shantytown, Baldspot set his box of ramen down on the ground, held up the styrofoam container, and said, 'Hyung, can't I have just one?'

In a gentle tone, without any browbeating, Bugeye said, 'They're ours, so let's leave half at home and cook up the other half at HQ.'

'Headquarters? Okay,' Baldspot said with a nod, and picked the box back up. 'If we leave the whole box at home, my dad'll get drunk and eat all of it with his friends.'

When the two boys were nearing the shack, they could hear Baron Ashura's drunken voice.

'We did all our work, so we deserve to get paid now, too. That's only fair.'

Bugeye saw Baldspot flinch, so he placed one finger to his lips and snuck over to the side door. The second shack that had been built onto the Baron's had become the boys' room. Bugeye hid his own ramen box beneath some folded-up blankets, and handed Baldspot his styrofoam container before motioning with his chin for Baldspot to go into the other shack. Baldspot led the way, with Bugeye right behind.

'Boys, you're right on time. I was just about to set the table ...'

Bugeye's mother looked happy to see them, but the Baron looked them over with suspicion.

'What's that you've got?'

'They handed it out at school,' Baldspot giggled.

'The church gave you that?'

'Oh, you know, it's one of those things,' Bugeye's mother said, recalling her days since the orphanage, 'where rich ladies come to have their picture taken.'

Baldspot opened his styrofoam container and, as if unable to stand it a second longer, shoved one of the *songpyeon* into his mouth.

'Dinner first, little man!' Baron Ashura said, rapping his knuckles against the boy's head, but Bugeye's mother stopped him.

'It's Chuseok. Let them enjoy their treats.'

She picked up one of the *songpyeon* and fed it to the Baron. Then, noticing the look on Bugeye's face, she quickly picked up two more and gave one to Bugeye and ate the other. The four of them munched happily on the treats.

'I'm sorry I couldn't make these for you myself. We just don't have the means. But we are getting paid today, aren't we?'

'It's like I just told you,' the Baron said. 'We all talked it over and agreed that since the private sectors are holding their purchasing day early because of the long holiday, the district sectors should get to do the same, that it's only fair, and we went to the management office about it. They said instead of working our usual shift this afternoon, we can sell off what we've collected.'

'That's great!'

Bugeye's mother was thrilled, but Baldspot was still pouting from the rap to the head he'd taken, and Bugeye kept stuffing *songpyeon* into his face with little interest in the matter. By the time his mother had set the table with their meagre meal of *dwenjang* stew and kimchi, a loud, whirring sound suddenly approached, and the plastic over the windows shook. Baron Ashura, who had just picked up his spoon, looked up at the ceiling and cursed.

'Why do those sons of bitches have to come around at dinnertime and make such a goddamn racket?'

Bugeye's mother latched the door to keep it from blowing open, and checked that the plastic sheeting over the windows was secure.

'Hurry up and eat,' she said.

Bugeye and Baldspot knew what that sound meant. They were itching to finish their dinner and get outside so they could watch the action. Twice a month, the city sent helicopters to fumigate Flower Island. Likewise, twice a day, after the bulldozers finished covering the garbage with a layer of fill dirt, cultivators sprayed insecticide. If not for that, the shantytown would have been so thick with flies that no one could have done their work properly. Back in Bugeye's old neighbourhood, the local administrative office used to send around a truck that sprayed for mosquitos. The mosquitos merely dodged the clouds of vapour and refused to die, but out here, the helicopters dumped a fog-like layer of insecticide, and the flies dropped like hail. The trash pickers had welcomed it at first, but later took to rushing away from the dumpsite and taking shelter inside their shacks without bothering to remove the dust or gas masks they wore while working.

As the helicopters churned overhead, the shantytown filled with a chemical stench. The boys, who'd been carefully gauging the right moment to make their escape, wolfed down the rest of their stew and rushed off to get a closer look at the helicopters. The Baron yelled for them to stay indoors, but they pretended not to hear him. The helicopters must have already passed by overhead, because the roofs and roads had turned a shiny black from dead flies. The only ones outside, of course, were the children of Flower Island. Excited, they all ran to the clearing from where the dumpsite was visible. The helicopter was hovering seven or eight storeys above the ground and spewing out insecticide left and right. It was low enough for the children to be able to make out the faces of the pilot and the city employee next to him. The employee, who wore a gas mask and a hard hat, waved both arms at the children to try to shoo them away, but the kids just waved back and shouted. He even tried throwing cans down at the kids to keep them from coming any closer.

'Hey, you little idiots! You wanna get sprayed, too?'

*

At nightfall, open clearings in every section of the shantytown lit up with bonfires. On top of stoves fashioned from oil drums sawn in half, meat was grilled, and stew fixings were mobilised from land, sea, and air. Now that the three-day Chuseok holiday was on the wane, the peak season for discarded items would be upon them soon, and the people of the shantytown would be able to gorge themselves for the first time in a long time on all sorts of holiday food waste. For the past two or three days, there had already been a growing amount of discarded food past its expiration date, no doubt from people cleaning out their refrigerators. City folk were always throwing out perfectly good food that they'd either been unable to finish and had let go untouched or had bought too much of and grew sick of eating. Once-frozen rice wrapped in plastic, now slimy and defrosted. Plastic bags, chockfull of shucked oysters. Whole fish, dried out and leathery. Hunks of meat, still frozen. Yellowed heads of cabbage that were still fresh once you peeled off the wilted outer leaves. Bucket upon bucket of fish heads and tails and guts thrown out of the fish market at dawn, and perfectly edible parts of the fish left over after the day's sale. At this time of year, every night was a feast for the people of Flower Island.

On holidays, when memorial ceremonies for family ancestors were held, those who rented rooms down in the village and commuted across the stream to the landfill would go into town and purchase simple food offerings, and even those whose families lived in the shantytown couldn't bear to set their ancestors' tables with food picked out of the trash, and would instead purchase *songpyeon* and even a small packet of meat from the shop near the dumpsite to make soup for the ceremony. The shopkeepers made a point of stocking *songpyeon* from the nearby town every year at Chuseok, just for that purpose.

As for Baron Ashura, he kicked off the holiday the same way he spent every other day—getting drunk in the clearing with the same guys he always got drunk with. He didn't return until the middle of the night, when the revelry had begun to settle down. Bugeye was awoken by the sound of someone pissing outside close by. *Goddammit,* he thought, *couldn't they pee somewhere further away?* He heard the Baron come through the door, belching nonstop as if he'd had far too much to drink.

Bugeye's mother exclaimed sharply, 'What kind of man are you?'

'Look, bitch, stop acting like you're my wife. What kinda man am I? I'm a trash picker, what's it to you?'

'Hand over the money. You think I don't know that you're blowing it all on alcohol and gambling?'

Bugeye heard Baldspot stir. He gave him a tap and whispered, 'Hey, let's go to HQ.'

Baldspot got dressed without saying a word, while Bugeye rolled up one of the blankets they shared. Baldspot folded up the other blanket and followed Bugeye outside. They left the shantytown with its rows of low roofs that barely concealed the sound of people coughing, babies crying, drunken fits, and fighting. The moon sat high in the sky, and the fields and river looked misty. The two boys made their way over the hill and down to the river's edge. As they were crossing the ridge of the former peanut field, Baldspot suddenly dropped into a crouch. This time, Bugeye didn't complain or pester him with questions, but simply followed suit.

In a low voice, Bugeye asked, 'Where are they? Which direction?'

Baldspot pointed wordlessly to the right. Bugeye squinted at the silver grass waving along the western edge of the river. He saw something—first one blue light, then two, then three and four. They were moving slowly. The next moment, the lights were moving quickly, then stopping, then moving again, making their way down the river away from the boys. And then, all at once, they disappeared. Baldspot swallowed hard and stood up.

'Hyung, did you see that?'

'Yup,' Bugeye said, and swallowed as well. Now he knew that Baldspot hadn't made it up. The lights were far too big to be fireflies, and they made no sound as they moved. Their gentle bobbing reminded him of dancing.

Bugeye remembered how Scrawny's mama had referred to the blue lights as the Mr. Kims, and he asked, 'Those are *dokkaebi*?'

'Told you so.'

Baldspot looked bewitched as he stared at the silver grass where the lights had vanished. Bugeye grabbed Baldspot.

'Let's follow them.'

'They say it's bad to startle them.'

Baldspot shook off Bugeye's hands and headed down to the hideout. Bugeye had no choice but to follow him, but he kept glancing back now and then.

As promised, Mole had scrounged up some scrap lumber, cardboard, and vinyl, and Bugeye had built a roof for the hideout in just half a day with Baldspot's help. Baldspot groped around on the table for the lighter and lit a candle. The candlelight made the hideout feel cozier than the shack. And they didn't have to put up with the night-long din of grown-ups cackling and fighting and singing, which sounded less like music and more like pigs being slaughtered. Even the sound of cars driving along the riverside expressway in the distance was just a soothing refrain. But best of all, the stench was gone, so their noses finally got some relief. The boys spread out their blankets and lay down. The space was even bigger than Baron Ashura's room; their entire gang could have slept there comfortably.

'This is nice,' Bugeye murmured.

'Hyung, can't we just live here, you and me?'

'We're only kids. They would never leave us be.'

Bugeye knew what he was talking about, because back in his old neighbourhood as well, whenever a parent suddenly died or took off, grown-ups would come from the local government office or the police station and take the kids away. After his father went missing, Bugeye's mother would swear to him as they lay in bed at night, *No son of mine is getting sent to some orphanage.* Bugeye couldn't have cared less what others thought about him or where he lived or any of that nonsense, and yet, why had he felt so ashamed each time he bumped into that girl in the middle-school uniform?

'Should we blow out the candle?' Baldspot asked.

Bugeye turned his head to extinguish the candle

on the desk. The hideout went pitch-black, but after a moment the plastic-covered windows began to brighten, and the moonlight seeped in. Just as they were teetering on the brink of sleep, someone coughed outside. Instantly awake and alert, Bugeye sat up in bed and strained his ears toward the sound. There it was. Another cough.

'Who's out there?' Bugeye shouted, waking Baldspot.

More curious than afraid, Bugeye opened the door and went outside. Baldspot followed and stood in front of the door. Bugeye walked all around the hideout, but all he saw was moonlight. He turned to head back inside when Baldspot pointed.

'Someone's coming.'

When Bugeye turned to look, there was a shadowy figure making its way towards them from the river's edge. Baldspot rushed over to Bugeye's side. It was a child. The child stopped some distance away and looked at them. Baldspot stepped out in front of Bugeye and addressed the child.

'You're one of the Mr. Kims, aren't you? It's okay. It's just us.'

The child came a little closer. Bugeye could make out the child's features now. It was a boy, about their age, with the same shaggy hair, stained shirt, and discarded blue jeans hacked off at the knee as all the other boys on the island.

The child came closer still and said, 'I know you two.

Grandpa told me to come find you.'

Bugeye realised then that the coughing sound he'd heard had been the child's grandfather poking around outside the hideout.

'What do you need us for?'

'Our family's sick. He says we'll get better if we eat something.'

'What do you eat?' Baldspot asked. 'We'll find whatever you need. We can find anything in the trash.'

The child hesitated and said, '*Memilmuk*.'

Bugeye and Baldspot stared at each other a moment. Neither of them were expecting the answer to be buckwheat jelly.

'We'll find it,' Bugeye finally said with a nod. The child bowed to them.

'Thank you.'

'But why do you look just like us?'

The child laughed quietly.

'Because we've been living alongside you all this time.'

'The people here make a living going through the trash. What do you guys do?' Baldspot asked.

'We farm. But it's much harder now.'

'The fields out there all belong to the farmers in the village across the stream. Where do you have room to farm?'

The child laughed again. He raised his arms and spun around in a circle.

'All of this is ours. Though it's harder with all that trash.'

Before leaving, the child added, 'Grandpa said that after all the people leave, we'll slowly put things back to how they were.'

'Don't worry,' Bugeye said, 'We'll find you some buckwheat jelly.'

'We'll bring it to you,' Baldspot added.

The child turned and headed down towards the river, his silhouette growing smaller and then disappearing. Baldspot and Bugeye realised that their hearts were racing and their legs were shaking, as if all of their strength had fled them.

'We just saw a ghost, right?' Bugeye muttered.

'Well,' Baldspot answered, 'he did say they've been *living* alongside us all this time.'

Those words had left an impression on Bugeye, too, but he was more surprised than frightened. And he couldn't help feeling a little sorrier for the child than he did for himself and Baldspot. The two boys returned to the hideout and lay down again. The moon was already tilting way over to the west.

*

When they awoke in the morning, a wet fog had crept up from the river to the base of the island, making the sky look very overcast. It was so chilly and damp that Bugeye and Baldspot slept curled up tight like two little larvae. The cold was probably what woke them. Bugeye pushed Baldspot, who was spooned right up against him, with his bum and said, 'Time to go home.'

'I don't wanna go home.'

'We need to get the ramen. We forgot all about it.'

'Oh! The ramen!'

Baldspot grabbed his baseball cap, put it on, and sprang up to go. The two boys walked over the hill through the thick fog and into the shantytown. Baldspot, who was walking in front, asked worriedly, 'Hyung, how are we ever going to find buckwheat jelly?'

'I'm worried about that, too,' Bugeye said. 'All they have at the shop is tofu and bean sprouts, and that sort of thing.'

'Can we ask Mum?'

Bugeye's fist went up towards Baldspot's head, but he stopped himself in time.

'We can never tell her. And we can't tell Mole or any of the other guys either.'

'But Scrawny's mama knows.'

Bugeye pointed at Baldspot and nodded.

'That's it! Let's talk to Scrawny's mama.'

The boys went back to the shack and snuck into their room so they could eavesdrop on the grown-ups in the other room. The night before, Bugeye's mother and Baron

Ashura had been fighting and raising a ruckus, but now they were all soft whispers and giggles.

'You boys back?'

At the sound of the Baron's voice, Baldspot's eyes widened and he shrunk his head down into his shoulders.

Bugeye whispered, 'I told you to shut the door quietly last night.'

The boys went into the other room. The Baron didn't look angry. His voice was loud, but his face was relaxed.

'You scamps! Little young to be sleeping away from home already. Were you out roaming around all night?'

'We slept in one of the empty shacks.'

The Baron looked at Bugeye as if he'd expected as much, while Bugeye's mother cut her eyes at the Baron.

'Who are you to scold them when you're the one who caused so much trouble last night? C'mon everyone, let's eat breakfast. I made seaweed soup with meat.'

The Baron threw his head back and laughed, and took two bills out of his back pocket and handed one each to Baldspot and Bugeye.

'The work team is going into the city today to have some fun. Buy yourselves something good to eat, and stay out of trouble.'

Baldspot and Bugeye gleefully tucked into their middle-class breakfast of moist white rice and seaweed soup and *chonggak* kimchi, and even a piece of grilled hairtail fish.

Whenever the grown-ups went across the river and into the city, they had to bathe a day in advance, or else they wouldn't be allowed into any decent establishments. If they got on a bus or went into a restaurant, the other people would plug their noses and look around, wondering where that awful smell was coming from, and when at last the epicentre was identified, everyone would back off to a safe distance or get up and change seats. Not long ago, a request had been made to the management office to install portable shower rooms. The residents of the island were still using a public bathhouse in the village across the stream, but the days leading up to major holidays like Chuseok were strictly reserved for the locals. Trash pickers weren't allowed in until the day of the holiday itself. Since it was the only place around for thousands of local residents to get a good scrub, it was high season at the bathhouse. Children and grown-ups would be packed in like sardines from morning to night, and since the women's section always had more kids, it took longer to finish bathing, and there were never enough water dippers to go around. Only after a great fuss and much scrubbing of their dirt-covered bodies did the people of the shantytown turn into normal, everyday locals, just like everyone else.

And yet, no matter how well they bathed, the smell would have worked its way deep into the fibres of their clothing, so the next thing they had to do was change into new clothes. It was impossible to keep anything clean and decent in a landfill shack. The clothes they wore as they worked and slept and relaxed at home had all been selected from among the rags they pulled out of the trash. There was always the odd foreign-made brand-name article of clothing to be found among the still-wearable items, but the smell was a constant problem. Once one of them found a decent set of clothing in the trash, they would take it to a dry cleaners near the bathhouse, where everyone from the island was a regular, and leave it there for laundering and safekeeping. Anyone who didn't own their own set of going-out clothes simply borrowed from what the others had left at the dry cleaner. Though they were always instantly identifiable on the intercity bus, once they lost themselves in the city crowds, they became indistinguishable from everyone else. Every now and then, one of the couples who'd gone into the city would return to the island still dressed in their going-out clothes to show off. Invariably, their crewmates would fail to recognise them, and the folks who'd been clinking soju glasses and cussing up a storm in the clearings would awkwardly switch to a more formal register or start throwing honorifics into their sentences.

Bugeye's mother had been to the bathhouse on her own a couple of times since they'd moved there, but though she pleaded with the Baron to take the boys with him when he went, he shook his head each time and said that he didn't want to have to scrub those two brats. Bugeye's mother was always saying how much better she would feel if she could take them there herself and give them a good scrubbing and get the smell of old trash off them, but she couldn't since they were too big to go into the women's side now.

Around noon, Baron Ashura's work team slowly began to gather in the clearing. They were already as giddy as children. They couldn't stop talking about how they were going to scrub off the dirt and get dolled up and head into the city, maybe see a movie, enjoy some *bulgogi* for dinner, with drinks of course, and then sing their hearts out at *noraebang*. One of the guys told the others about how some of the people from the private sector had gone with the truck owner to some cabaret or hostess bar, and got sloshed and blew all of their earnings in one night. He described how the men had ironed their wrinkled money out flat before tucking it into the inside pockets of their jackets. 'Know why?' he added. 'Because otherwise, man, the bills won't fan out right when they whip all that cash out of their pockets.'

Since it was a day off for the pickers, every part of the landfill, with the sole exception of the area in front of the shop, was quiet and tranquil. There was no heavy equipment or trucks making their way up and down, and nearly half of the trash pickers had flown the coop for the day, leaving the paths and clearings of the shantytown bereft of grown-ups. Bugeye and Baldspot had left the path, the box of ramen tucked under Baldspot's arm, and were headed for the hideout when they heard someone call to them from behind. Bugeye turned to see Mole and two other boys walking towards them, each carrying a plastic shopping bag.

'What's that? Instant noodles?' Mole asked, giving the box an indifferent poke. 'You got that from the church, didn't you?'

Bugeye peeked into the other boys' bags.

'You're not planning to make that Flower Island stew again, are you?'

Bugeye didn't hide the derision in his voice when he referred to the stew Mole had made for them last time from discarded fish. The adults called everything cooked with foodstuffs scrounged from the landfill 'Flower Island stew'.

'Watch it, man. Don't you know who I am? I'm the youngest member of the Co-op!'

The Environmental Co-operative was the crème de la crème of all of the private truck sectors, the one the Baron was forever envious of, as it covered the U.S. military bases, the factory districts, and the private residential areas. Along with three districts south of the river, the permit fee for the Co-op was many times higher than anywhere else. The military bases were known for ruthlessly tossing out food the second it was past the expiration date, regardless of whether it was still edible or not, and there were other items, from clothing to military supplies, in such good condition that the pickers couldn't bring themselves to sell it all off by weight. As for the factory districts, those were a paradise of scrap metal, plastic, Styrofoam, vinyl, cardboard, and other recyclables. Mole was able to work on the second line thanks to his father and older brothers, who had been the first to arrive on Flower Island. Mole was carrying two plastic bags stuffed with small boxes.

'You're all gonna think you're in heaven today, thanks to me.'

The boys took Mole's bragging in stride. When they reached the hideout, the first thing Mole did was give the roof poles a light kick, tap the plastic door, and walk all around so he could get a good look at the place, behaving as if he were the rightful owner.

'The roof looks good. But didn't I say to add a window on each side?'

'Whatever, man. Don't talk to me about windows. It took a whole day just to make that door.'

'Fair enough. Weather's getting colder anyway.'

They left the door wide open, went inside, and sat in a circle.

'Hey, this is *nice* … Whose blankets are these?' Mole asked, as he lay back with his arms behind his head.

'They're ours,' Baldspot said with a giggle.

'We slept here last night,' Bugeye explained. 'The grown-ups were fighting …'

Mole gave him a knowing laugh and said, 'Your mum and his dad, right? Don't sweat it. A lot of kids here don't live with their parents. My dad lives in one place, and my hyung and I have our own place.'

Though Bugeye was put off by Mole's assumptions, the customs of Flower Island dictated that Bugeye had to laugh it off. Just as Bugeye had expected, Mole was different from the other kids. He looked like he could get by on his own without grown-ups' help; he would never find himself sent to an orphanage. Two more boys appeared in the doorway. Bugeye was familiar with the two who had accompanied Mole, but these two were new to him.

'Oy, Cap'n, long time no see.'

The boy who spoke was tall, and looked like he might be older than he appeared. He gave Bugeye a dirty look as he sat across from Mole. Bugeye had told Mole he was fifteen so he could stand his ground against him, but he found out later that the boy giving him the stinkeye was fourteen, a whole year older than Bugeye's actual age. After everyone was seated, the belated introductions began.

'This is the new kid,' Mole began, pointing at Bugeye. 'I told you all about him last time. His name's Bugeye, and he works, too, like me.'

'Bugeye? That's a fucked-up nickname … Not that mine's any better. Everyone calls me Stink Bug.'

Mole chuckled and added, 'His nickname can go both ways. You can call him either Stink or Bug.'

The boys all laughed. Bugeye was annoyed at how the kid had so rudely told him he had a fucked-up nickname, so he made a point of laughing extra hard and smacking the ground with his palm. Stink or Bug or whatever he called himself looked caught off guard by Bugeye's reaction: even though he'd shown no hesitation in revealing his nickname, he immediately started to scowl. They all went around and introduced themselves by their nicknames. The two boys Bugeye had met before were chubby-cheeked Toad and Scab, whose face was crusted over from eczema. Then there was Beetle, a short, dark-skinned kid the same age as Baldspot. Even though Bugeye had earned his nickname from a cop back home who'd smacked him with rolled-up police reports, he still felt that, compared to the other boy's nicknames, there was something dashing, manly even, about his own.

Stink Bug lowered his head and looked up menacingly at Bugeye.

'You laughin' at me?'

Everyone got quiet. Mole looked back and forth at the two of them as though he was enjoying himself. Bugeye stopped laughing.

'C'mon man, I was only laughing because you were laughing.'

'Bullshit.'

As soon as the kid scrambled up off the ground and made to kick at him, Bugeye leaped up. Mole jumped between them.

'If you're gonna fight, then at least take it outside and make it a real fight.'

The boys spilled out into the yard in front of the hideout. Bugeye was no stranger to fights, having been through dozens back home, and he knew that boys like Stink Bug, who were quick to anger, always had a weak spot. He stood at ease, not bothering to adopt any particular boxing stance, his hands loose at his sides, while Stink or Bug or whatever started showing off his footwork, raising his clenched fists aloft and bouncing around like he was looking for an opening. Bugeye never dragged out his fights. He always threw the first punch, and could zero in on any weakness and lay the other kid out in just a few moves. When Stink Bug came at Bugeye with a high kick, Bugeye didn't dodge out of the way, but instead grabbed Stink Bug's leg with one hand and socked him in the face with the other. Stink Bug fell flat on his bum, and Bugeye followed with two swift kicks to the ribs. Stink Bug curled up on the ground, and gasped and hacked for air. It was almost disappointing how fast the fight had ended. Bugeye crouched down and patted Stink Bug on the back.

'Hey, man, you okay?'

'Get him some water,' said Mole.

Beetle poured some water from the plastic jug and tried to hand it to him, but Stink Bug shoved his hand away, scrambled up, and ran towards the field. Beetle tried to go after him, but Mole stopped him.

'Leave him alone, he's just embarrassed. He'll come back soon enough.'

Bugeye felt proud that he'd demonstrated to Mole and the others that he was not to be trifled with, but outwardly he acted as if it were no big deal.

'What's the point in fighting?' he said. 'We should've just laughed it off.'

'Well, that's why we call him Stink Bug. He's always making a stink over every little thing.'

Since the boy in question was gone, the other kids felt free to laugh. Mole pulled four small boxes out of the plastic bag. He opened one to reveal several cans and a chocolate-coloured packet. Toad craned forward to steal a peek.

'What is that?'

Scab leaned in knowingly and said, 'I've had one of those before. It comes from the U.S. army base. It's got all sorts of stuff.'

Mole tore open the packet without comment. Several more packets of various shapes were inside. There was a round piece of chocolate covered in silver foil, crackers in foil packets, butter, cheese, jam, square pieces of gum, even a few cigarettes, coffee, cocoa, sugar, milk, and more, but the boys simply crowded around Mole and stared down at the items. Mole fished two can-openers out of the bag. One had a longish hole drilled through one end, while the other had a curved edge like a gardening hoe. Before opening the cans, Mole took a quick glance around.

'Hey, if we've got any newspaper or cardboard, bring it here.'

Beetle scampered away and came back with some scraps of cardboard they'd been saving for kindling. Mole slowly opened the cans. One contained a chunk of ham; the other, chicken noodle soup.

'This is called a C-ration. We get them sometimes in our hauls.'

Mole opened up all four boxes of C-rations, grouped the items together on the cardboard, and distributed them equally. The four round chocolate pieces were snapped in half, and a piece was given to everyone, followed by three pieces of gum and two cubes of sugar each. The canned foods were all dumped together into their one cooking pot. They splashed in some water, set the pot on top of their makeshift stove, and lit the fire; soon, a mouth-watering aroma filled the air. When the pot came to a boil, they added the instant noodles. They could tell just from looking at it that they'd cooked up something amazing. Mole served the food. They lined up in front of the pot, holding an empty can each and a pair of disposable chopsticks that had been used far more than once.

Bugeye slurped up a chunk of meat and a mouthful of noodles, and asked Mole, 'Why do people throw away perfectly good food?'

'Beats me. This stuff is delicious.'

'I wish I could eat this every day,' Baldspot giggled, as he polished off his can of soup and ladled a second helping into it.

The boys were happy. Mole sat back, the perfect image of a captain, puffing away leisurely on a cigarette and gazing contentedly at the boys as they slurped down their food. When the feast ended, the boy they called Scab suddenly pulled something out of his pocket, as if he'd forgotten all about it until then, and held it out.

'I brought this for HQ.'

Mole looked the item over and gave one of the buttons a push. A tinny electronic melody started to play. A brick wall appeared on the screen, and as a small round dot began to ricochet back and forth, the bricks disappeared one by one.

'This is a brick-breaking game,' Mole said. 'But only pre-schoolers play it. Nowadays everyone is into Super Mario.'

'What's Super Mario?' Scab asked.

'I found one at work once,' Mole said. 'It was broken, though, so I just threw it away.'

Mole handed the game back to Scab, and the youngsters—Beetle, Baldspot, and Toad—sat together and took turns playing it. Mole and Bugeye went up the hill behind the hideout and looked down at the sunlight sparkling on the river's surface.

'Have you been to the city yet?' Mole asked.

'I used to live there, but I haven't been back since we came here.'

Mole's mood seemed to sour at hearing that Bugeye

had lived in the city.

'Hey, man, you said you lived in the slums. I'm not talking about that, I mean downtown, as in, the middle of the city. I ate a hamburger there once.'

'I only passed through. There was a department store and a movie theatre and a bunch of bars.'

'The place the grown-ups go is just the outskirts of the city. Let's you and I cross the river someday and go downtown for real.'

Bugeye laughed.

'And do what? Without money, we can't do anything.'

*

The big, round full moon floated over the river. Bugeye and Baldspot snuck out of the hideout. They knew where they were going without having to say it out loud. They crossed the farm and the hill, and headed for the field on the other side of the shantytown. They could see a single speck of light way off in the distance and hear the occasional bark. As they approached the house, the dogs in the greenhouse began barking noisily. The door opened, and they heard the voice of Peddler Grandpa.

'Come right in, boys.'

Bugeye and Baldspot went inside. Scrawny yapped fiercely before leaping into Baldspot's arms and wagging her tail. The other dogs all pressed their noses to his feet and whined. Scrawny's mama was in the middle of cooking dinner.

'The little uncles are back!' she exclaimed. 'Where've you been all day? Did you eat?'

'Of course they haven't eaten,' Peddler Grandpa said. 'Sit down and eat with us.'

'No, thank you,' Bugeye said honestly. 'We've been snacking all day, so we're not hungry.'

'We made rice cake. At least have a taste.'

Scrawny's mama plated up two types of sweet rice cake—steamed *sirutteok* and *songpyeon* stuffed with sweetened sesame seeds. While father and daughter ate dinner, the two boys feasted on rice cake, and even the dogs munched away happily at their own dinners. It had been a long time since Bugeye had had a taste of *sirutteok* with its topping of mashed sweet red beans—perhaps not since one of his birthdays long ago, when he was very young.

Baldspot asked Scrawny's mama out of the blue, 'Do you know where we could buy memilmuk?'

Scrawny's mama stared speechlessly at Baldspot, her spoon in mid-air, and finally asked, 'Buckwheat jelly? What on earth are you going to do with that?'

Since Peddler Grandpa was there, too, Bugeye gave Baldspot a sly kick under the table, but Baldspot didn't seem to catch on. He blurted out, 'We ran into the littlest of the Mr. Kim *dokkaebi*. He said his family is sick. And they'll only get better if they eat memilmuk …'

Peddler Grandpa pretended not to have heard a word and just kept right on eating, but Scrawny's mama set her spoon down and scooted her chair closer to Baldspot's.

'Sounds like you met the youngest grandchild. The Mr. Kim family lives the way we used to in the old days—three generations under one roof. It's easy to find memilmuk in the marketplace.'

Grandpa Peddler turned and said, 'Shall I run out and buy some now?'

The three of them stopped talking at once and looked at him.

'It's a holiday,' he said, 'If you're going to do something nice for them, may as well be tonight.'

He chugged a glass of water and stood with a grunt. Bugeye followed him out.

'Grandpa, would it be okay if I went with you?'

'Sure, it should only take about twenty minutes or so to cross the river and come back.'

Baldspot and Scrawny's mama began boiling leftover food for the big dogs in the greenhouse, while Peddler Grandpa and Bugeye got in the truck. There was a well-trodden dirt path, so, though it was a bit bumpy, they were soon passing the little shop and the office, and turning onto the big paved road that the garbage trucks used. They took the bridge that Bugeye and his mother had crossed when they first came to the island, but instead of merging onto the riverside expressway, they headed for a small two-lane highway. The road turned to softer asphalt and was even lined with trees. It was the first time in months that Bugeye had gotten away from Flower Island.

As he drove, Peddler Grandpa muttered, almost as if to himself, 'I guess there really is such a thing as a Mr. Kim *dokkaebi*.'

'They said they've always lived alongside us.'

Peddler Grandpa glanced over at Bugeye.

'So that story, about *dokkaebi* liking buckwheat jelly, is true after all. I thought my daughter was making it all up.'

'… So did I.'

The town appeared in the distance. Way out at the centre of the vegetable fields and rice paddies, electric lights glowed, two and three-storey buildings rose up, and a newly paved road led to a main street lined with shops and restaurants, off which branched smaller roads packed with homes. The truck made a left-hand turn off the main road into a surprisingly large parking lot, where the tiny alleyways of an outdoor marketplace appeared. Peddler Grandpa parked the truck and made his way into the warren of alleys, turning this way and that, hurrying past small shops that sold freshly pressed sesame oil, general stores that sold all manner of odds and ends, and restaurants serving *gukbap*, and then came to a stop in front of one shop in particular. The marketplace was closed, but every few doors a shop would be open: inside, you'd see either three or four fellow vendors clustered together, enjoying their holiday meal and drinking makkolli, or else one elderly man or woman watching television alone. The shop that Peddler Grandpa was searching for turned out to be a stall that sold pre-made side dishes. With everything from seasoned greens and cooked bean sprouts to marinated tofu, it was the sort of place that people shopping for groceries in the evenings would always made a point of stopping by. It was apparent to Bugeye that Peddler Grandpa must have searched his memory and figured that this place was likely to sell buckwheat jelly.

'You sell *muk*, right?' Peddler Grandpa called out. 'Got any buckwheat jelly?'

The auntie who ran the shop poked her head out of the door.

'We're out. But who eats that on holidays anyway? Come back tomorrow.'

'I need it tonight.'

'What'd you do? Bet a plate of *muk* in a game of cards?' She cackled at her own joke.

The last thing she would have expected to see on Chuseok was someone shopping for buckwheat jelly. She abruptly shouted across the alley to another shop.

'Hey! You sell buckwheat starch, right?'

The male shopkeeper poked around for a bit and then held up a plastic sack. He gave it a little shake as if to ask whether that was what they were looking for. Peddler

Grandpa went over and checked the label. The store had five sacks of buckwheat starch in total, and he picked each one up in turn before saying, 'I'll take 'em all.'

'All of them? What, are you opening a buckwheat jelly factory or something?'

Peddler Grandpa added a crate of makkolli, as well, making ten bottles in total. He and Bugeye divvied up the parcels, and carried them all back to the truck.

'I forgot that you can make your own,' Grandpa said. 'It's the same as making glue. You boil the starch until it thickens up. Back in the old days, that's how we made mung bean and acorn muk.'

'I haven't had memilmuk in a long time.'

Peddler Grandpa nodded.

'I bet. There are a ton of things we don't do anymore these days.'

They headed back to Flower Island. From a distance, the island looked like one long, low hill. The moon hovered just above the crest of the hill, and to the right of the field that was visible from the dumpsite, the lights of the village on the other side of the stream glowed against the side of the hill.

'Grandpa, have people always lived on the island?'

'Of course, I was born there. There used to be a big village there. Everyone was paid to move across the stream instead, but then a lot of people said that place wasn't liveable anymore either, and left.'

Bugeye missed his old neighbourhood. He redrew the alleyways of the hillside slum in his head.

'Whoever heard of a place being unliveable?' Peddler Grandpa went on. 'If you don't have money, then everywhere is unliveable. Around here, we might have to put up with a few flies, but we make money, don't we? Once the weather cools off, the flies and mosquitos will go away, and it'll be liveable enough.'

He headed for the bridge that would take them across the stream.

'I'm so glad you boys have started visiting. My daughter used to go out and wander around by herself. Those jerks would call her crazy and throw rocks at her.'

Bugeye listened without comment.

'She's been like that since she turned twenty, ever since her mama died. Folks say it means the spirits have caught her and that we have to call in a shaman and hold a ceremony to bring her back. Her mind still comes and goes sometimes, but at least she's better than she used to be.'

The truck headed uphill, and passed the office and the shop again.

'I guess it's no different from living with flies ... how those, whatchamacallit—*things* or spirits or whatever—live with us, too. Aren't you boys afraid?'

Bugeye shook his head.

'No, I think it's fun.'

How could anything be scary, compared to waking up every morning to the same unchanging stench, the dust and the flies, the monstrous dump trucks pouring out hideous-looking objects of all shapes and origins? Now, even when the tip of his rake pulled out the rotted trunk of some animal, he simply kicked it away and buried it beneath other items. People threw away so many things that by the time the objects lost their shape and decomposed into smaller and smaller and more complex parts, they became strange and curious objects that bore no resemblance whatsoever to whatever the machines in the factories had originally spat out. Bugeye gazed down at the moonlit grass and nearly murmured, *I want to fly away.*

The truck pulled up to the front of the house, and the dogs resumed their barking. This time, they weren't warning barks so much as a chorus of welcomes. Bugeye knew this was so because of the whines and whimpers wending their way between the barks. When he and Peddler Grandpa carried the stuff they'd bought into the house, the elderly crippled dogs were the first to run over and sniff the bags. Baldspot and Scrawny's mama took the bags from them.

'What is all this?' Scrawny's mama asked.

Bugeye answered for Peddler Grandpa. 'Buckwheat starch. He said all we have to do is boil it.'

'Ah, great! I know what to do.'

Scrawny's mama emptied an entire bag of the starch

into the big plastic mixing bowl she used for making kimchi, added water, and stirred it together with a rice paddle. Then she took it outside and poured it into the kettle on top of the makeshift stove and brought it to a boil. In the meantime, Peddler Grandpa couldn't wait, and went ahead and cracked open a bottle of makkolli; he poured himself a bowl and downed it at once. Scrawny's mama poured the boiled starch back into the mixing bowl and brought it inside, where she patted it out flat and placed it on the counter.

'It'll harden up as soon as it cools—wait, Dad, you're drinking already?'

'I had to make sure it tastes okay. After all, what's buckwheat jelly without some makkolli to go with it?'

It had taken just about an hour and a half for them to get back from the market, boil up the buckwheat starch, and let it cool. If they'd had a square pan, the muk would have come out in neat little rectangles, the way it was supposed to, but since they only had a bowl, it came out domed instead, like part of the moon had been sliced off. Nevertheless, when it was divided into blocks and sliced up on the cutting board, it was indeed a perfect batch of memilmuk. Scrawny's mama carried the bowl of sliced-up muk on top of her head, while Bugeye and Baldspot each carried a plastic bag stuffed with bottles of makkolli. They were headed out the door when Scrawny started yipping and yapping, intent on going with them. Peddler Grandpa picked the little pup up and watched them leave.

'Make sure you ask them to fix your head,' he said to Scrawny's mama.

The moon was already hanging way up at the top of the sky, and the whole world had turned silver. The moonlight was different from electric lights: it hid the ugly things, and turned the river and trees and grass and stones and everything else close and familiar. The three of them waded through the tall grass and headed for the bend in the stream. The moonlight on the grass made them feel like they'd stepped into a new world. Bent branches and short shrubs caught at their ankles, and each time the silver grass, as tall as the boys themselves, brushed their cheeks, they shivered from the chill of the night dew that clung to the blades. They saw tall trees standing in a circle, the moonlight glimmering behind the branches.

When they reached the yard in front of the shrine, they set down the bowl of muk, uncapped the bottles of makkolli, and arranged everything neatly along the wooden ledge. Scrawny's mama picked up one of the bottles and went over to the willow tree, where she took a big mouthful and sprayed the base of the tree with the makkolli. After she'd nearly emptied the bottle doing this, her body began to twitch and she collapsed onto the ground, her shoulders rising and falling as she retched. She lay there for a long while, her arms and legs still writhing, and then just as suddenly sat right back up as if nothing had happened. Baldspot had experienced her fits several times now, and calmly held her hand, but Bugeye was startled all over again, despite having witnessed it once before. He had a vague sense that her fits did not follow any set schedule, but rather grabbed hold whenever the feeling came over her.

'Come!' she said, waving both hands in front of her. 'Come and enjoy these offerings!'

She was peering into the woods as she spoke. Baldspot and Bugeye saw blue lights moving between the trees. Then, all at once, people were there, thronging the edges of the clearing, their voices a low murmur, as they kept a proper distance. Scrawny's mama pressed her hands against the boys' backs and urged them back towards the river. Only then did the shadowy figures approach the shrine and help themselves to the buckwheat jelly and the makkolli. A small shadow came towards the three of them. Baldspot recognised the child.

'We brought you memilmuk,' he said.

'Thank you.'

Just as before, the child bowed at the waist.

'Is your whole family here?' Bugeye asked.

'Yes, that's my grandfather and my grandmother and my father and my mother and my dad's older brother and his wife and my dad's younger brother and his wife and my mother's brother and my mother's sister and my dad's sister and my other aunt and my older cousin and my big sister, and then there's me, the youngest.'

The child recited each family member's title as if he were chanting some sort of spell.

'Do you recognise me?' Scrawny's mama asked. 'Mr. Kim is your father, right?'

The child laughed and said, 'In our family, everyone is Mr. Kim. Auntie, can Granny Willow speak through you?'

'I'm her right now.'

'Then have some memilmuk with us.'

'That's okay. I had myself a nice, refreshing drink of makkolli.'

The child returned to his family, and the sounds of murmuring voices and eating and drinking continued. After a while, the child reappeared from between the trees.

'Come on, my family would like to meet you.'

Baldspot led the way, followed by Bugeye and Scrawny's mama. There seemed to be about twenty people in the clearing; they were assembled in front of the shrine as if they were taking a family portrait. A man dressed in faded grey coveralls and a baseball cap printed with the words 'New Village Movement', looking no different from any other middle-aged man from the neighbourhood, stepped forward and addressed them.

'I'm the child's father. We were sick with something and unable to do much, but thanks to you we got better.'

The white-bearded grandfather standing behind him nodded.

'Look at this,' he chuckled. 'My arms and legs work now.'

He pinwheeled his limbs. Dressed in an old suit with cotton pants that puckered at the knees, he, too, looked just like any other grandfather you would see in the neighbourhood. A middle-aged woman in baggy, floral print pants and a clashing shirt with a kerchief tied around her head was the child's mother. She turned to Scrawny's mama.

'Please look after us, Granny Willow,' she said.

'You're good, reliable folk,' Scrawny's mama replied. 'You must look after each other.'

'Come visit us sometime,' the child said to Baldspot.

'Wait, you live around here?' he asked in surprise.

The child laughed again.

'Flower Island has always been our home.'

'The food was delicious,' the grandfather said. His voice was filled with energy. 'Time for us to get back to work.'

With that, they were suddenly all in motion, slipping away one by one through the trees. Spots of blue light appeared briefly and then faded. Scrawny's mama and the two boys stood stock still, speechless.

As if having just returned to his senses, Bugeye muttered flatly, 'What the hell was that? They look just like our neighbours. Where are they going now? To pick through the trash?'

'They said they're farmers, silly,' Baldspot said with a giggle, and Scrawny's mama nodded.

'Granny Willow says this island belongs to them,' she said.

They left the forest, walked back through the silver grass, and returned to Scrawny's house, passing piles of discarded electronics as they went.

4

As autumn deepened, the work grew harder. Homes were being heated again with coal briquettes to ward off the cold nights, and with the return of the ten-day-long kimchi-making season, not only the first-line workers but even the second-line ones were hard-pressed to find any items worth salvaging from the trash. Non-stop waves of spent coal briquettes and withered cabbage leaves buried every last bit of vinyl, plastic, aluminium, cardboard, and scrap metal. There was no exception for any of the districts: at least half of everything that came in was cabbage leaves and coal ash.

'That's how it goes,' the Baron kept reminding his team. 'Goodbye flies and mosquitos, hello coal!'

When the morning shift ended, the bulldozers that brought in fill dirt rolled over the coal briquettes, flattening the earth back down and blanketing everything in a layer of white ash. Faces that were once a shiny black from dirt and grease now turned white, as if everyone had been dredged in flour.

On the evening of the first snow, Bugeye was helping his mother to sort out and deliver the items she'd pulled from the trash. They had come down to the sorting area at the base of the dumpsite and were dividing the items up into large vinyl sacks when Peddler Grandpa came over to them from the line of parked motorcycles and trucks.

'Anything good today?' he asked Bugeye's mother.

'It's been nothing but cabbage,' she said with a sigh. 'But we did get a lot of cardboard at least. You should take some cardboard and vinyl.'

The peddlers, who acted as middle-men, carrying off whatever items they could on their motorcycles or in small trucks, bought whatever they wanted regardless of whether it was purchasing day, and so whenever the trash pickers were in need of a little extra, they could usually make a few bills from them.

'Put all those cans and plastic in the truck for me, kid,' Peddler Grandpa said to Bugeye.

Bugeye dragged the five sacks they'd collected off to the side. After everything was weighed on the scales and Peddler Grandpa paid Bugeye's mother, Bugeye slung the sacks over his shoulder and carried them to Peddler Grandpa's truck.

Peddler Grandpa got behind the wheel and asked, 'You done for the day?'

'I was sorting stuff.'

'They're looking for you.'

'Scrawny's mama?'

'I think she's with your little brother.'

Bugeye nodded and ran back to his mother to tell her he was off to find Baldspot. Since she'd made him work all day from the crack of dawn, and he was always left to his own devices anyway when it came to dinner, she turned a blind eye and continued with what she was doing, throwing him only a quick glance in acknowledgement. When the truck headlights turned on, Bugeye saw something flying around in the air. He hadn't felt it through the several layers of work clothes and the cap he wore, but it had begun to snow. Bugeye cried out, his voice trembling with the barest edge of excitement.

'It's snowing!'

'So it is,' Peddler Grandpa said as he steered the truck away. 'At least it won't be too heavy, since it's the first snow of the year. It's hard on everyone when it snows a lot.'

On their way from the dumpsite to Scrawny's house, the snow grew a little heavier. But most of the flakes that landed on the windshield melted right away and turned to water drops. The barking and yapping of the dogs was like a signal for the front door to open and Scrawny's mama and Baldspot to poke their heads outside. The yard was speckled with snow.

'Is it a special day?' Bugeye asked.

Scrawny's mama set the table with small plates of food

and explained, 'I put up kimchi for the winter today. Since there's only two of us, I didn't make that much. But I figured I may as well make a big batch of memilmuk while I was at it.'

'The Mr. Kims are going to love it,' Baldspot said, his voice half giggles, as it always was when he was in high spirits. 'I can't wait to see that boy again.'

The table was set with the tender, yellow inner leaves of cabbage, leftover kimchi seasoning, and slices of boiled pork belly. Scrawny's mama sat down at the head of the table and poured Peddler Grandpa a bowl of makkolli. She started to pour some for herself as well, but he snatched the bottle away and, even while asking, 'Sure you can handle this? Weather's pretty bad tonight,' he was already pouring her a bowl, too. Together they gulped down their brew. Then she and the boys headed out—she carrying the big mixing bowl of muk on her head, the boys toting the bottles of makkolli—and made their way towards the patch of woods near the bend in the stream. The slim branches and the dried silver grass were damp to the touch, and the exposed sandy earth was covered in a layer of snow. Just as she had before, Scrawny's mama walked straight over to the old willow tree, took a swig of makkolli, and sprayed it on the trunk. Her shoulders rose and fell and her body twitched, but this time she didn't fall backwards or go into convulsions; her voice alone changed and took on a serene tone.

'Mm, that hits the spot!'

She placed the bowl of memilmuk directly on the ground in front of the shrine, lined up the bottles of makkolli, and called out towards the tall grass.

'Come on now! Come get your offerings!'

There was a murmuring in the darkness, and shadowy figures emerged. This time, the *dokkaebi* did not keep their distance but came right up to Bugeye, Baldspot, and Scrawny's mama. There was the father in his New Village Movement cap, the mother in her baggy floral pants with the kerchief around her head, the grandfather with his white beard, the grandmother, the father's older brother in his faded suit, the mother's brother in his army reserves uniform, the younger uncle and his wife, the mother's sister and her husband, the father's sister and her husband, the cousins, the older brothers and sisters, and finally, the youngest of the entire family, the child. The family crowded around the bowl of buckwheat jelly, sending a slight breeze over the three of them as they passed by. All at once, the yard in front of the shrine where they stood was filled with people. Each time one of the Mr. Kims came close to them, it felt like nothing more than a cool breeze brushing their skin. And though their faces were a little dark, their skin wasn't blue or red or anything like that. It was somehow no different from running into neighbours you'd known a long time.

The child's father came over to Scrawny's mama.

'Thanks to you, Granny Willow, our whole family is better now,' he said.

'Please eat your fill.'

'How've you been?' the child asked Baldspot and Bugeye. 'We've been terribly busy.'

'Doing what?' Baldspot asked.

'Bringing in the autumn harvest. Now we can rest until next year's first full moon.'

'Eat up, you,' Scrawny's mama said.

At her urging, the child bowed his head, slipped back into the crowd of grown-ups, and ate some memilmuk. The three of them watched with satisfaction as the Mr. Kims ate and drank their fill. After they'd enjoyed the muk and drunk all of the makkolli, they lined up again, bade farewell to Scrawny's mama and the boys, and slowly retreated from the yard in front of the shrine. The child came back over to Baldspot.

'Would you two like to come see our neighbourhood?'

'Can we really go with you?' Baldspot asked with his usual giggle.

'Just follow me.'

The child walked into the tall silver grass the grown-ups had vanished into, and Bugeye and Baldspot followed without a second thought. No sooner had the dried leaves of the overgrown grass grazed their cheeks than everything went dark and then slowly brightened to a kind of milky glow, though they still could not make out anything. A thick fog surrounded them. The child, who was walking ahead, flickered in and out of view, and from that they could tell that the fog was very gradually starting to thin. The light wasn't bright or clear as at midday; instead it was a soft, pastel light, like moonlight. To the right a river flowed, and across the river was an open field, and beyond the field was mountain after mountain, all of different heights. Behind the two boys, an enormous hill rose up like a cliff, high and imposing, right above the river's edge, and in front of them was a sandy inlet, low hills, and sorghum swaying in a field. A winding, curving path was lined with large, lush willow trees. At the end of the path was a small village thick with bamboo. They could see thatched roofs here and there, and at the top of a hill was another village. Bugeye hurried to catch up with the child.

'Where are we?' he asked.

The child answered as always with a laugh.

'Can't you tell? This is Flower Island.'

'This is the same island?' Baldspot asked as he looked around in all directions.

'Yes, this is what it was like in the old days.'

'Flower Island in the old days?'

'That's what I'm trying to tell you. This is where we live.'

They stopped to look down at the river: there was another neighbouring island with its own low mountain and lush grove of trees. A small sailboat drifted slowly past.

A mama cow and her calf nibbled at the grass in a field near the river's edge, and right on the banks where flowers bloomed, ducks were taking off and landing and dabbling their beaks in the water.

Bugeye took a long look around before saying, 'I've never seen that island before.'

'People blew it up. Our relatives who lived there moved away long ago,' the child said. 'We'll probably leave this place someday, too.'

The adults who'd been walking ahead all disappeared into their separate houses. The child led Bugeye and Baldspot into the courtyard of an L-shaped house with a thatched roof. The child's oldest brother was in the yard chopping firewood, his mother was in the kitchen putting something on to boil in the big iron cauldron, his father was sitting on the narrow side porch smoking a pipe, and his sisters were piling the laundry into a basin and carrying it down to the river. The cow and her calf, the ducks and the sailboat, the family—they all kept repeating the same movements over and over, like a set of moving tableaus on replay.

'What happened to all the trash, and our shacks?' Bugeye asked.

'You can't see them right now, but they're there, too. Always.'

The child turned back the way they came and pointed.

'See how thick the fog is. This awful fog has been

covering our whole village more and more often.'

The child pointed towards the opposite end of the village, which was blanketed in the same thick, smoke-like fog.

'We can't go over there anymore. A lot of them left, and now it's just our family.'

The child opened the door to a storage shed; the inside was as big as the grand hall of a Buddhist temple. Small sacks hung from the rafters and crossbeams, filling the entire space from wall to wall and ceiling to floor.

'This is what we did all autumn.'

'What? Is that all rice?'

Baldspot's jaw dropped as he gazed up at the sacks.

'Those are flower seeds. Our family harvested them. When spring comes, we'll sow them wherever there's soil on Flower Island.'

The child led Bugeye and Baldspot back the way they'd come. Bugeye looked back: the hills and mountains and fields and village looked very quiet and very far away, like a painting of a moonlit landscape. The child stopped at the edge of the fog.

'Farewell. We'll meet again.'

Bugeye and Baldspot were suddenly swept back into the fog. They pushed their way back through the tall silver grass, only to find themselves lying in the yard in front of the shrine.

'So you boys finally came to,' Scrawny's mama said.

'It's cold. Better get up. Time to go home.'

Bugeye and Baldspot stared at each other in bewilderment.

*

The weather grew colder and the days shorter and shorter, making the working conditions that much worse, and causing the pickers to grumble about their languishing wages. They had to work in darkness until late into the early-morning shift, and by five in the evening it was already dark again. Once evening did fall, people gathered in front of the shop and in every clearing in the shantytown to drink hard, and their bonfires grew bigger and burned longer into the night. The hubbub they made was no different, but small conflicts that arose while working were quicker to grow into full-blown fights. Whenever a fight grew, the amount of broken glass and scrap metal and other rough implements lying around meant that the argument would not stop at grabbed collars, but was sure instead to end in spilled blood.

Few days went by without an argument between the Baron and Bugeye's mother because of the Baron's unflagging enthusiasm for cracking open another bottle— which he claimed was necessary for him as crew leader to ensure the camaraderie of his workers—and his propensity for gambling late into the night. He usually drank and played card games of Go-Stop with his work crew or the crew leaders from neighbouring districts; but on this particular day, the drinking party had grown to include the leaders of the smaller units from the private truck districts. The private districts were run like individual companies, and the owners of the trucks, who were essentially the CEOs, had a monopoly on all of the trash their trucks collected. They split the profits thirty-seventy with the unit leaders and their work crews, whom they hired as employees. The permit fees for the private sectors were expensive, but the items discarded there were of such high value that those workers made far more money than those assigned to the district dumps. The unit leaders were mostly in their thirties and forties, and were spoiled by their relative wealth. Judging by the way they would all get together and head into town en masse to scare up some fun each time another purchasing day rolled around, they were thick as thieves, to boot.

There was one downside to Baron Ashura's district sector, and that was having to crush all those aluminium cans, which brought in the same amount of money as plastic. Flattening out the smaller items, like beer cans and food cans which fitted in your hand, was annoying enough; but even the larger items, like oil drums, aluminium bowls, pots and pans, and other sundry metal containers, had to be crushed and flattened one by one so that they could be easily sorted and sold in bulk. That meant hammering them with a mallet or crushing them underfoot, which took a long time. But it just so happened that the Environmental Co-operative team, which collected trash from the U.S. military bases, owned a compactor; for them, the work took mere seconds. The Baron went in search of the Co-op's unit leader for their work crew. The Co-op had converted a container box into a private office behind the management office. The Baron stepped inside the container to find several unit leaders from various teams sitting around drinking soju.

'Well, look who's here,' one of the men said.

'What're you doing here? All the big stuff's been collected already.'

The men made comments to try to get under his skin, but the Baron ignored them. He gave a nod to the unit leader he was looking for.

'Bak, you mind if we talk for a second?'

Swarthy, thickset Bak stayed seated where he was and said, 'What's with the serious face?'

'It's no big deal. I just wanted to ask you something.'

Bak pulled a face, but followed the Baron outside.

'I have a favour to ask,' the Baron explained. 'I was wondering if my crew could share the use of your compactor.'

Bak smirked.

'I guess you could bring your stuff over and use it. After we're done with it, that is. But you know, that ain't going to look too good. Why not just sell us your aluminium instead?'

The Baron thought it over. There were indeed times when they handed items over to the private districts. But they always ended up losing half, or at a minimum one-third, of what they would have made if they'd sold it straight to the recycling plants or to peddlers instead.

'I would have to talk it over with my crew first,' the Baron demurred. 'What about charging us a small fee each time we use it instead?'

Bak chuckled and patted the Baron on the back.

'Son of a bitch. That's not a bad idea. In that case, drinks are on you tonight. Can you get some soju from the shop?'

With that, the Baron headed over to the shop, bought ten extra-large bottles of soju, and toted them back to the office. The drinking party that had started without him had all but run out of booze, but there were still plenty of snacks to go around.

Visibly delighted at the arrival of more soju, one of the younger unit leaders offered some meat to the Baron and said, 'This stuff is called turkey. We get to eat it before those Yanks do.'

His lips and fingers were slick with grease from the shredded turkey meat and thinly sliced pork sitting on wax paper. The table was strewn with oranges, each one stamped with the name of the place where they'd been grown, as well as plums preserved in syrup, and other treats. Bak had probably told the rest of the men why he was bringing them soju. As he drank, the Baron, who was prone to showing off, felt his mood start to lift.

'We may not make as much as the Co-operative sector or the downtown areas, but our permit fees are the highest of all of the district sectors. Puts my mind at ease to know my workers can make ends meet.'

'Seems our lordship here has raked in quite the income.'

'Well, you know, all that cabbage from the kimchi season was a big headache, but once Christmas rolls around, we'll be back on easy street.'

'Which sector are you?' someone asked.

Bak answered before the Baron could. 'South-east part of the city, up towards the northern end, I think.'

'That's a decent area. Two big marketplaces, and isn't it basically the heart of that part of the city? Lot of small factories, too, I bet.'

As the unit leaders all chimed in, the Baron slowly forgot that he'd barged in on someone else's party.

'We're the best of the district sectors,' he crowed.

'Hey, hey,' Bak said, changing the subject. 'Let's not leave our good crew leader out and only play amongst ourselves. C'mon, get the cards out.'

'Yeah, let's get a taste of some of that district money.'

The snacks and booze were pushed to one side, and one of the unit leaders took out a deck of *hwatu* flower cards.

'There're too many of us for Go-Stop, and it takes forever to finish a game. Let's play Jitgoddaeng or Seotda instead.'

'Seotda! The rules are simpler, but it's more exciting.'

'Okay, but let's decide on the values of the cards first. If we do it later, we'll end up arguing about it.'

'How much should we ante?'

'100 won is too stingy, and 1000 won is too steep, but 500 won should be just about our speed.'

'So, if it's 500 to ante, 500 to stay in the game after you get your first two cards, 500 to swap one of your cards with one from the deck, 500 to stay in the game again with your new card, and another 500 to raise, then the minimum pot is 2,500 won.'

Everyone was talking at the same time as they set the rules. Stones from a *baduk* set were used as chips, and everyone placed two 10,000-won bills under the board in exchange for forty *baduk* stones. If anyone ran out of stones, they could buy more from someone else by producing more cash. The Baron saw no danger in playing. He started out with an okay hand and was doing all right in the betting, but then his luck turned, and after a few rounds he was out of money. He lost even more money for a couple more rounds before finally pulling a *jangddaeng*, two high maple cards. He'd already lost a million or more won, which was the equivalent of blowing about half a month's earnings. In the next round, two of the men folded after pulling new cards. The remaining four each flipped one of their new cards over, and one more folded. Then, when the bets were raised, another folded. Only the Baron and Bak were left. Just then, the Baron caught the fleeting moment in which one of the men who'd folded quickly slipped a card into Bak's hand.

'Hold on, just what the hell d'you think you're doing?'

'What, indeed? Hurry up and cut the deck.'

'You switched cards!'

'Ha, you're crazy. Stop acting like a child, and let's see your cards.'

The Baron angrily slammed his hand down to reveal the two maple cards. Bak grinned and slowly turned over his own hand: *gwangddaeng*. The big, round, white sun printed on each of the cards shone into the Baron's eyes, prying them wide open. While the Baron was picking up the March sun card and the August sun card, trying to figure out which one had been switched, Bak stuck both arms out to rake in the pile of *baduk* stones. The Baron lost his temper and flipped the table. *Hwatu* cards and *baduk* stones and soju glasses and snacks went flying in all directions.

'You no-good son of a bitch! Are you crazy? You wanna die?'

Of all the men there, Bak was the biggest bruiser and most ready for a fight. He grabbed the Baron by the collar, hoisted him up, and headbutted him in the face.

The Baron fell on his bum, eyes spinning and seeing stars, blood running from both nostrils. He groped around on the floor and grabbed something and then, as he stood, he drove the object into Bak. Bak looked down glassy-eyed at the knife sticking out of his stomach. He looked around at everyone in the room, the look on his face seeming to say, *How'd this knife get here?* He grabbed the Baron and they fell to the floor together. The Baron's upper body was drenched with blood spurting from Bak's stomach. The other men hurriedly rolled Bak over and pulled him off the Baron.

The unit leaders from the Co-operative sector ran to the management office to summon an ambulance and call the police. The whole place filled with the loud wailing of sirens and flashing red lights of the arriving police car and ambulance. Bugeye's mother missed all the commotion, but Bugeye and Baldspot squeezed through the crowd in time to see the Baron being stuffed into a police car in handcuffs. The spectacle drew not only the people who were outside drinking in the clearings throughout the shantytown, but even people who'd been fast asleep in their shacks. And yet, accidental deaths were not uncommon, and patrol cars screeching up because of some brawl was likewise commonplace, and so no one was very surprised. Few nights went by without at least a couple of people getting three sheets to the wind and throwing punches at each other.

The Baron had already been carted away by the time Bugeye's mother heard the news from the woman next door, but all she did was stare down at the bridge that led to the riverside expressway and did not say a word. Worried, Bugeye pushed open the door to the Baron's room to check on her, but she turned her back and quickly wiped her face.

'It's just as well,' she said with a sigh. 'He drinks too much, every single day, and when he isn't fighting, he's out somewhere gambling.'

Bugeye closed the door, but he could still hear his mother muttering to herself.

'*Aigo*, I have the worst luck.'

Bugeye and Baldspot lay next to each other in the dark and didn't speak. After a while, Baldspot exclaimed with a giggle, as if it had only just then occurred to him, 'Dad got arrested!'

Bugeye was feeling sad for his mother, but Baldspot seemed almost gleeful that his own father had been taken away.

'Does it make you that happy to see your father arrested?'

'He's a bad man. He is. My mum left, and then the next woman after her couldn't take it and left, too. And now your poor mum … He's bad. He hits me on the head every day.'

'Did the other guy die?'

'Probably. There was a ton of blood.'

Bugeye thought about his father. He did not know how long his father had to stay in that re-education camp or whatever it was, which claimed it turned people into new people before sending them back out into the world, but he thought about what it meant to become a new person. He'd wondered the same thing back when he first heard what happened to his father and had asked the mailman about it. The mailman said it meant following the straight and narrow. But what was the straight and narrow when you lived in a garbage dump? People bought things with money, did whatever they wanted with those things, and threw them away when they were no longer of use. Maybe folks like him had also been thrown away when they were no longer of use.

After a long silence, Baldspot swallowed hard and asked Bugeye, 'Hyung, you get punished real bad for killing someone, right?'

'Death penalty, I bet.'

'What's a death penalty?'

Bugeye shook his head in the dark and changed his answer.

'That man wasn't hurt that badly. He'll get stitched up at the hospital and'll be better in no time. Your dad will be back soon.'

Baldspot lay there quietly for a moment before rolling away from Bugeye. His constant sniffling started to bother Bugeye, so Bugeye asked him, 'Are you crying?'

'Yeah, I can't stop thinking about my mum.'

Bugeye suddenly felt choked up. He rolled towards Baldspot and patted him on the shoulder.

'Go to sleep now. It'll all be better in the morning.'

The next morning at dawn, Bugeye awoke, got dressed for work, and waited outside for his mother, but the light stayed off in her room and she did not come out. Maybe she was still asleep or not feeling well. When he got to the sorting area, Hard Hat had the crew all gathered together.

'Your mum's not coming?' he asked Bugeye.

'She's sick. Could I work on the first line in her place?'

'No can do. You're underage.'

Hard Hat was standing in as crew leader for the Baron, and as he glanced around, one of the women from the second line spoke up.

'Of course she doesn't have the heart to work today. I guess I'll just have to take her place.'

'What? Why do you get to? I've been here longer than you!' said one of the men from the second line.

'She and I are both women. That's why.'

The other women from the second line started to raise a racket, but Hard Hat held up his hand and motioned for them to stop.

'Enough! Knock it off, everyone! She can take the first line for today. Now, let's get going. The trucks are coming in.'

Hard Hat jumped into the headlights of the oncoming

line of trucks and ran ahead, shouting, 'A little further, a little further!'

Bugeye's mother didn't show up for work until late in the afternoon. Her face looked haggard, but she was probably reluctant to miss out on the higher-priced items that came from the factories and construction sites, and decided to make a late run for those items at least. Bugeye watched her work: her back looked like it would break from the strain. Before, whenever her rake caught on some scrap metal or rusted rebar that refused to budge, the Baron would come running to help her free it. This time, Bugeye found himself rushing forward to help his mother, but before he could reach her, Hard Hat was already there, smoothly plucking out the piece of scrap iron that had stayed her rake and tossing it behind him. Bugeye picked it up and set it aside.

'Did you hear?' Hard Hat asked.

'Hear what ...'

'The guy they took to the hospital, he's not dead, but he lost his intestines. They're calling it attempted murder, so our crew leader won't be getting out any time soon.'

Bugeye's mother raked away at the trash and did not respond. She fished out a scrap of vinyl and a plastic window frame, and tossed it behind her.

'Maybe you should go visit him.'

Bugeye's mother finally paused and stared at Hard Hat. 'We're not family, so how can I?'

141

'What do you mean you're not family?' Hard Hat thoughtlessly said the first thing that came to his mind, 'Just tell them you're his sister, or his live-in girlfriend …'

As his voice trailed off, Bugeye's mother replied calmly, 'I mean we're not *legally* family.'

Hard Hat sidled up closer to Bugeye's mother, as if he'd liked the sound of her answer.

'I hear he's at the local police station. You should take the kids. Just tell them you live together, or that you have a—what's it called?—common-law marriage? The cops know how it is out here, so they'll let you see him.'

Bugeye's mother dropped her rake and sank down into a squat. Hard Hat gestured sympathetically as he kept trying to explain.

'Do you get what I'm trying to tell you? Think about it. Not to be blunt, but it's not like you'll be getting any sort of alimony or compensation. I bet he has money stashed somewhere. A cheque account, at least. If you look after him while he's in jail, he's bound to help you out in return when they throw him in prison for good.'

Bugeye's mother looked up at Hard Hat.

'Where do I go?'

'You'll have to go to the management office first and find out what's going on, and then you'll be able to take the boys with you to the police station. You should leave tomorrow morning.'

Bugeye listened to every word of their conversation.

When they returned home late in the evening, his mother prepared dinner for Bugeye and Baldspot, but only ate a few bites herself.

'Don't go to work in the morning,' she told Bugeye.

Bugeye already knew the plan, but he kept eating and didn't respond.

'You boys have to go into town with me tomorrow.'

'Just take Baldspot,' Bugeye said cautiously.

His mother thought it over for a moment and then turned and lay down without saying another word. Bugeye quietly cleared the table and took Baldspot into the other room. As soon as they sat down, Baldspot asked, 'Hyung, why am I going into town?'

'To see your father.'

'I don't want to. I'm not going.'

'It's going to be a long time before you see your father again, man. Is that what you want?'

'I hope he never comes back.'

'Well, Mum is taking you, so you better go with her.'

They spread out their blankets in the dark and lay down. Just like the day before, they were quiet for a long time.

'Hyung, do you ever think about that place we went with the *dokkaebi*?'

Bugeye didn't just think about it sometimes. Very often, while working away at the mounds of garbage, he would picture the scene by the riverside, and have to stop and look around, only to be scolded by his mother and the Baron to get his head out of the clouds.

'I guess. Did we dream it?'

'No, I spotted them a few times after that, as floating blue lights. Can't we go live there?'

Bugeye felt a vague yet unmistakable stab of fear as he thought about how to answer Baldspot's question.

'We're people, and they're *dokkaebi*. That's like asking why we can't live with fish.'

Baldspot rolled over and let out a long, very unchildlike sigh.

'I guess we have to keep living here with the trash then.'

The next morning, Bugeye's mother brought buckets of water over and scrubbed herself clean, and then gave Baldspot a good scrubbing as well, changing the water in the basin twice before it ran clear. They both changed into their going-out clothes and headed to the management office so she could inform them that she was off to visit the Baron in jail. The employee gave her a pitying nod and asked, 'Did you remember to bring your ID card?'

Bugeye's mother kept opening her wallet and double-checking that her ID was inside, while the employee rummaged around in a desk drawer and pulled out a business card.

'This is the detective in charge of the case. If you talk to him, he'll arrange a visit.'

Bugeye's mother took the business card, tucked it

carefully into her wallet next to her ID, bowed deeply from the waist, and left the office looking much brighter and more confident than when they'd entered. She and Baldspot walked down the dusty unpaved road and across the bridge. They caught an intercity bus into town, where they found their way to the police station, asking for directions as they went. At the front door, she showed the detective's card to the guard on duty.

'I'm here to see this person.'

The young, uniformed guard checked the name on the business card and said, 'Go to the security division.'

Bugeye's mother wandered up and down the hallways swarming busily with people until she finally found the door marked Security Division and cautiously opened it. Another young man, a detective this time, dressed in a leather jacket, was sitting facing the door. He frowned and said, 'What is it?'

'I, uh …'

He took the business card from her and shouted over the partition behind him.

'Detective Yi! Someone here to see you.'

A well-built middle-aged man in a shirt and tie appeared, and looked Bugeye's mother and Baldspot up and down. He sniffed the air, as if to say he could tell who they were from the smell.

'You're from Flower Island? Come this way.'

Behind the partition was an ordinary office with

desks and filing cabinets, but many of the seats were empty. There were only two other people there besides the detective. They looked over once, but didn't interfere.

'Sit down.'

Bugeye's mother and Baldspot sat down timidly, perched right on the edge of the folding chairs, their heads hanging down. The detective mentioned the Baron's name to the colleague sitting across from him.

'Is that investigation still going?'

'It just started. Probably three or four more days.'

'What a pain in the arse …'

'Stop complaining. That place is a gold mine.'

'Yeah, a gold mine for trouble …'

Detective Yi turned back to Bugeye's mother.

'What's your relation?'

'I live with him. This is his son.'

Her voice was barely audible, but the detective seemed indifferent, as if he'd seen it all before.

'Common-law marriage, you mean. Typical. I'm always warning you blue-collar types about that sort of rough living. That arsehole you're with needs to grow up.'

He called someone in another department, and gave a long explanation. He sounded irritated as he said, 'There's only so much to investigate. We know the facts of the case, and we already have statements from the witnesses. He'll change his tune once he meets the family. This is my jurisdiction, so that's why I'm asking for your help.'

He stood with a grunt.

'Come with me.'

He took them over to the holding cells, took Bugeye's mother's ID, and filled out a visitation form for her, handed it to the uniformed officer, and then explained to Bugeye's mother: 'Next time, this will all be automatic. You can come straight here and hand in one of these forms.'

As the detective turned to leave, he reached his hand out to pat Baldspot on the head, but the boy quickly ducked out of the way. The detective stood there a moment, his hand hovering in mid-air.

'Why, you little—you're as rotten as your father.'

Bugeye's mother and Baldspot entered the visitation room. Since it was just a small county jail, the visitation room was nothing more than a table and four chairs in a glorified broom closet next to the holding cells. After a brief wait, the guard brought the Baron in, handcuffed, and looking very rumpled and ragged. They all sat down at the table.

'You came to see me,' he said to Baldspot, sounding entirely unlike his usual self.

Bugeye's mother asked, 'Are you okay?'

'Yeah, sure, I guess. What're you doing here?'

'Don't worry about things at home. I'll look after the boy.'

'Sorry.'

He sounded depressed, like he was already a changed

man. They were both quiet for a moment, and then Bugeye's mother spoke again.

'Is there anything I can do for you? Maybe bring you some food …'

He chuckled.

'The food here is actually pretty good. Don't worry about that, but you could put some money in my commissary account. I left something at the office.'

'What did you leave?'

'My bankbook and my seal for signing papers. I'll write you a letter of proxy so you can get it for me. And if I were you, I'd use this chance to pay the permit fee to move over to one of the private sectors.'

'Thank you. But shouldn't we hire a lawyer?'

For the first time, the Baron looked angry.

'Goddammit, we don't need those sharks. I got drunk and did a bad thing. Why complicate it?'

The guard, who had been taking notes the whole time, stood and said, 'Visiting time's over.'

As the Baron turned to leave, Baldspot burst into tears. The adults were startled by the boy's reaction. His father stared down blankly at the boy for a moment, then said:

'She's your mama now. Be good …'

He left, and Bugeye's mother tried to calm Baldspot down, but the boy's shoulders shook from the force of his weeping.

5

Christmas was coming. The other kids Baldspot's age were spending all of their time crowded into the church school, but for some reason or other Baldspot insisted on helping Bugeye with work. Kids weren't officially allowed near the dumpsite, as it was too dangerous, but Baldspot stayed glued to Bugeye's side anyway, from afternoon until late into the evening. The only shift he skipped was the early-morning one. He turned out to be quite adept at carrying baskets full of scavenged items, separating the items into different categories, and stuffing it all into sacks.

'Go home and play,' Bugeye's mother would say, 'Your big brother and I are working.'

As far as she could see, now that his father was gone, the little guy figured he had to earn his keep, and she felt sorry for him. She told him repeatedly to go home, but Baldspot didn't say a word and just kept gathering up the items that Bugeye had tossed back and putting them into baskets. Hard Hat, who'd taken over as crew leader, scolded them at first, warning Bugeye's mother to keep Baldspot away from there, but eventually he gave up as well and told her to make sure that all he was doing was helping Bugeye and to keep him off the trash heaps. Bugeye's mother fashioned a clean towel into a mask for Baldspot, and stuffed his hands into a pair of work gloves, the palms of which were coated with a red laminate. When she was done, he looked like a proper little trash picker. By the time the afternoon and evening shifts were over, it was as dark as midnight. Ever since the Baron had been carted off, Bugeye and Baldspot had stopped sneaking away to eat, and began joining their mother for meals.

That night, Bugeye's mother had just finished setting the table.

'Where's your little brother?' she asked. 'Go find him quick.'

'He was with us earlier. I didn't see him leave the site.'

'He must've gone to the church. They've been giving away all sorts of things lately.'

'But he hasn't been there in a long time …'

'Well, I'm going into town tomorrow. His father's being transferred to the prison, so I should visit him before that happens.'

She sat down at the table and gazed at Bugeye.

'I wonder what's become of your father,' she said, her voice trailing off. 'Anyway, things should get better soon. I'm planning to switch to the private sector.'

'With what money?'

His mother brightened and said, 'I'll find a way.'

The two of them went ahead and ate without Baldspot. Afterwards, Bugeye went into their room and lit a candle: there, in the middle of the floor, were Baldspot's gloves, mask, and torn work shirt. As he picked up the gloves, something occurred to him, and he left the shack. He hurried along the path that cut through the centre of the shantytown and passed the new rows of motley shacks thrown together from plastic and cardboard. Past the field covered in dry grass and over the hill he went, then across the ridged paddies and down towards the river's edge. When he arrived at the hideout, it was dark, and there was no sign of anyone about. Where had that kid gone? Bugeye lit a candle, sat down and covered his legs with the sleeping bag that Mole and his gang had stashed there, and waited blankly, little puffs of down from the torn sleeping bag floating around him.

As it turned out, Baldspot had left the dumpsite by himself, stopped by the shack to drop off his work gear, and then headed to the hideout alone. The whole time he'd been working, he had not been able to get the Mr. Kims and their mysterious village out of his mind, and had decided he just had to find that child again. Since it was after dark, he knew the *dokkaebi* would appear, as they always did, in the silver grass that grew on the banks of the river near the hideout. He hunkered down in front

151

of the hideout and peered this way and that into the dark. He'd been sitting there for quite some time, with no sign of their tell-tale floating blue lights, when suddenly a shadow appeared on the slope below. It slowly made its way towards him and revealed itself to be the child. Baldspot ran towards it in excitement.

'I couldn't wait to see you!' he shouted.

The child stepped neatly to the side, dodging Baldspot's outstretched arms, nearly causing him to fall flat on his face. The child kept its distance, and greeted Baldspot with a smile.

'I thought you might be looking for me,' the child said.

'I want to go back to where you live.'

The child laughed, and didn't respond.

'Grandfather told me to show you something good,' the child said instead.

He gestured for Baldspot to follow, and vanished. A blue light appeared up ahead, so Baldspot ran to catch up to it. It kept gliding away from him, then stopping, then gliding away again. Baldspot climbed the hill, but instead of taking the path back to the shantytown, he followed the ridgeline, making his way up and down along the mountain's curves. He eventually came around the corner of the shantytown and found himself right next to the dumpsite; the last work shift had been over for some time, and all of the heavy equipment had been taken away. No one was around. The blue light didn't stop. It floated right over to the middle of the trash, which was covered with a damp blanket of fill dirt. Bits and ends of discarded items stuck out here and there, and Baldspot's feet sank in where the earth had not been tamped down well. The child's shadow reappeared.

'There's something here,' the child said.

Baldspot squatted down and dug up the soil with his bare hands. The tip of a plastic sack tied shut with a ribbon emerged. He gave it a tug, and it pulled free from the soil like a tiny sapling. 'What is this?' he asked as he turned to look at the child, who was now suddenly far away and speaking to him from across a great distance.

'Take care. We'll meet again.'

The child faded, then vanished. Baldspot untied the ribbon and groped inside the bag. He could feel something wrapped in newspaper and something else that felt like soft, smooth fabric. He tore the newspaper with his fingernails and ran his finger over whatever was inside. It felt like small rectangles of paper tied together. He looked around at the darkness and hurried back the way he'd come.

Back at the hideout, Bugeye was dozing off under the sleeping bag when he heard someone tiptoeing around outside. He pulled open the plastic door and called out, 'Baldspot? Is that you?'

Baldspot let out a short shriek. 'Hyung! You scared me.'

'What're you doing just standing there? Where were you? You skipped dinner.'

'The light was on. I didn't know it was you … I was afraid to go inside.'

They went in and sat down. Bugeye pointed at the bag. 'What is that? Food?'

'I don't know. I found it and brought it back here so I could take a closer look.'

Baldspot turned the bag upside down and dumped out the contents. Sticking out of the newspaper that he'd torn with his fingernail was a stack of bills neatly bound together with a paper strip. Bugeye and Baldspot tore at the rest of the newspaper: there were five stacks of cash altogether, one of which was a little smaller than the others. They stared at each other and then down at the money, their jaws hanging open in bewilderment.

'One of these should be about one million won,' Bugeye said. 'And this smaller bundle is American money. I've seen it before.'

'A h–hundred million?'

Baldspot scooted back and mumbled under his breath. He looked terrified, as if he'd done something wrong.

'Did you find this in the trash?' Bugeye asked.

Baldspot nodded.

'I saw the little boy again. The *dokkaebi*. He said he had something good to show me. I followed him, and found this.'

Bugeye picked up the other item that had fallen out of the bag: a dark-red pouch tied shut with a cord. Inside was a gold necklace, a tiny gold pig, a gold tortoise, and a pair of rings set with stones. Baldspot scooted back over. He looked more drawn to the gold than to the money. He gingerly picked up the pig and tortoise, and held them in his palm.

'Heyyy, these are pretty. Let's give them to Mum.'

Bugeye snatched them back and put them in the pouch. He tied the cord tight and stuffed it into his jacket pocket.

'We better hide 'em. They're easy to lose.'

'No! I want to give them to Mum,' Baldspot whined, but Bugeye tried to appease him.

'Don't worry, I'll let you give them to her. But I'll keep them in my pocket for now so we don't lose them on the way back. I'll hand them back to you right before we get home.'

Baldspot turned the matter over in his head. If he told his mother they found jewellery, then, knowing her, she would almost certainly insist on reporting it to the management office. Back when she was a little girl growing up in an orphanage, whenever one of her classmates' belongings went missing at school, they all pointed the finger at her. She thought there was nothing more shameful than being accused of stealing, and her fear of being labelled a thief only increased after Bugeye's father had been put away more than once for burglary. On the other hand, Bugeye figured, since cash bore no mark of ownership, and moved from pocket to pocket and could therefore belong to anyone, surely even his mother would feel no qualms about keeping it.

'Hyung, let's hurry up and go home.'

'All right.'

The two boys cautiously made their way back to the shantytown, and when they arrived at their shack they went into their own room first. They put their ear to the door of the other room: it sounded like Bugeye's mother was already asleep. Bugeye put the jewellery pouch and the stacks of cash back in the plastic bag, tied it up tight, and hid it beneath the cardboard box that they stored their clothes in.

'If we give the pretty stuff to Mum,' he whispered to Baldspot, 'she'll get mad. She doesn't like other people's things. So let's keep that stuff to ourselves.'

Baldspot frowned and asked, 'Why won't she like it?'

'She'll want to give it back to the owner. If you tell anyone about this, we'll get in huge trouble.'

'I won't tell. Ever.'

To ensure that Baldspot's lips were sealed, Bugeye added, 'If anyone finds out, they'll put us away.'

'Like my dad?' Baldspot's eyes widened.

Bugeye gave him a firm nod.

'We'll go into the city tomorrow, or the day after.'

'Across the river? Okay!'

Baldspot's voice was so loud that Bugeye had to put his hand over his mouth.

Bugeye woke automatically at dawn, but, recalling how his mother had said she planned to go into town that day, he pulled the covers back over his head. He'd fallen back into a deep sleep when his mother cracked open the door.

'I'll be back later,' she whispered. 'Heat up the leftover rice for the two of you. You don't have to work today.'

'Okay,' Bugeye murmured from beneath the blanket.

By the time he remembered to tell his mother about the money they'd found, she had already left. He meant to sleep a bit longer, but he found himself suddenly wide awake. No sooner had he begun to think about what they should do with the money and jewellery than his heart was racing like it had the night before. He wanted to keep the gold, but it wasn't like cash; he was sure it would prove to be nothing but trouble. His father had referred to that sort of thing as 'stolen goods', and he was pretty sure his father also said that he'd gotten caught before while trying to sell such goods, or while holding onto them. Bugeye decided the best thing to do would be to take the gold to Scrawny's house and give it to Peddler Grandpa. He thought carefully about what Baldspot had told him. It must have been a gift from the Mr. Kims in exchange for treating them to buckwheat jelly. Though Scrawny's Mother deserved a share, she wasn't always in her right mind, so it was best to give it to Peddler Grandpa. He could be trusted. Bugeye's plan was to hide the cash for now and give it to his mother later in private. But first, he wanted to have some fun with one of the bundles.

He checked to make sure Baldspot was asleep, and took out the bag that he'd hidden beneath the box of clothes. He went into his mother's room and pulled back a corner of the linoleum. He bent back the sheet of cardboard underneath and cleared away the layers of Styrofoam and plastic until the bare earth was exposed. Then he grabbed some tools from the cubby next to the front door and started to dig. When the hole was deep enough, he took the jewellery pouch and one of the bundles of money out of the plastic bag, tied it tight, and stuffed the bag into the hole. After refilling the hole, the dirt was mounded up on top, so he tossed the extra dirt outside, stamped the ground down flat, and put all of the layers of plastic and Styrofoam and cardboard back in place until the linoleum was once again flat and back to its original condition. He put the jewellery pouch in one pocket and the cash in the other, and gave them both a firm pat. At last, his heart had stopped racing and he couldn't help smiling. Baldspot came into the room then, his face still puffy with sleep. Bugeye was in high spirits as he heated up the stove and put the leftover rice in a pan with some chilli paste and kimchi to stir-fry for their breakfast. They stuck two spoons into the pan of fried rice and plunked it down on the table. When they were done eating, Bugeye said, 'Let's go have some fun today.'

'In the city? Hooray!'

'By the way, Mum said she doesn't want the jewellery.

What do you think of giving it to Peddler Grandpa instead?'

'To him? Not Scrawny's mama?' Baldspot asked, wide-eyed.

'She's not always in her right mind, so she'll just lose it. We'll give it to Grandpa for safekeeping instead. Don't tell anyone. Understand?'

'All right, all right. We'll give it to him.'

The boys passed the shop and the office, and headed through the field. Baldspot was so excited that he kept skipping and jumping as he went, but Bugeye walked with his head down, convinced that everyone's eyes were fixed on him. When they reached Scrawny's house, the dogs barked, and Scrawny's mama looked outside.

'Is Grandpa around?' Bugeye asked.

'He was here a minute ago. Check out back.'

While Baldspot was busy hugging Scrawny and the other dogs, Bugeye went behind the greenhouse where discarded electronics and other sundry items lay in piles. Peddler Grandpa and two women in masks and hats were breaking apart the electronics, and picking out the parts that were still usable.

'Grandpa ...'

Peddler Grandpa stopped working and stood up.

'What're you doing here?' he asked. He pulled off his hat and his military goggles, pulled his mask down below his chin, and walked over to Bugeye. 'Am I needed in the house?'

'I brought something for you.'

Peddler Grandpa followed Bugeye with a grin.

'A gift for me? Well, ain't that something.'

When they were a safe distance from the two women, Bugeye pulled the jewellrey pouch from his jacket pocket.

'Please take these.'

Grandpa opened the pouch and peeked inside. His face hardened.

'Where did you get these?'

'We found it in the dump.'

The tension in Peddler Grandpa's face softened, and his smile returned.

'Oh, then that means they have no owner. Why didn't you give it to your mother?'

'She said she doesn't want it. There was some money, too.'

Peddler Grandpa put the pouch in the pocket of his coveralls.

'I guess that old saying about befriending *dokkaebi* is true,' he said with a laugh. 'All sorts of things can happen. Go on in and have some lunch.'

Peddler Grandpa stood and watched as Bugeye ran towards the house. Scrawny's mama poked her head outside, Scrawny held tightly in her arms, and called for the boys to come in and eat, but Bugeye waved at her and ran off with Baldspot in tow. Bugeye felt so unburdened, he thought his feet might leave the ground and he'd sail off into the air at any moment.

*

Bugeye took Baldspot into town. They had to be careful, since Bugeye's mother was also there visiting the jail. Baldspot was wearing his torn baseball cap, his grey padded jacket shiny with grease and dirt, and his baggy jeans with half the legs hacked off to fit him. He'd been wearing the same clothes every day since the start of autumn, and though it was a given that they would be dirty by now, the smell coming off them was beyond foul. Bugeye's clothing was no better. He wore jeans and a thick brown jacket with fake fur on the collar, both of which had been fished from the trash. His mother had found the clothes last autumn and washed it all before he wore any of it, of course, but they had been through a straight month and a half now of digging through trash by day and lolling around on the ground by night.

The two boys crossed the bridge over the stream and caught an intercity bus into town; as soon as they boarded, the other passengers plugged their noses and frowned and got up to move seats, and the driver caught their eyes in the rear-view mirror and loudly ordered them to move all the way to the back. Because Bugeye had paid attention when the grown-ups went into town, he knew the first thing they would have to do was buy a fresh set of clothes. Bugeye asked directions to the marketplace, and headed straight for the cluster of clothing stores. When the plump shopkeeper who'd been dozing off in her chair saw them come in, she plugged her nose and exclaimed with a laugh, 'Goodness! Now there's a smell that'll wake a person up!'

Bugeye chose a checkered shirt and a black duck-down parka for himself, and then selected a similar shirt and a blue parka for Baldspot.

'Boys, you live over on Flower Island, don't you? You're going to need a whole new everything, from the underwear on up.'

If they'd come with Bugeye's poor mother, she would've asked how much it all cost, and turned tail and run, but Bugeye whipped out his cash and changed into his new shirt and pants on the spot, and stuffed a shopping bag with new underwear and socks as well. He bought Baldspot a new sky-blue baseball cap, but the scamp refused to throw out his old one and stuffed it into his back pocket instead. It went without saying that they threw away everything else they'd been wearing. The shopkeeper kept her nose plugged as she placed their old rags in the trashcan. Their rags would make the rounds and eventually find their way back to Flower Island.

The boys headed to a shoe store a few steps away and bought themselves new sneakers. Baldspot kept stamping his feet on the ground to test out his new shoes and bringing the sleeve of his new parka to his nose to sniff it. Bugeye felt like he'd finally turned into one of those normal middle-class boys that he'd once been so familiar with, and he felt proud.

They asked directions to the public bathhouse. This time, the old lady at the ticket counter did not plug her nose and turn her head. Since it was the middle of the day, they had the whole bathhouse to themselves. Baldspot was so enchanted by the hot water that rained down from the overhead showers that he could only stick one hand under and laugh. When Bugeye shoved him all the way under, Baldspot jumped and shrieked at how hot it was. The water in the tubs, which had been filled in the morning, had cooled to just the right temperature. Had the grown-ups been there, they would have opened up the tap and overflowed the tub with scalding hot water, but Bugeye was perfectly content and sank down until the water was up to his chin. As the muscles in his groin warmed and relaxed, he felt the urge to pee, so he went ahead and did it right there. A pool of yellow spread out around him. *Who cares? It's just us*, he thought.

'Aren't you coming in?' he asked Baldspot, who was playing around, scooping the water with a plastic dipper.

'No, it's too hot.'

'It's not that hot. It feels really good ...'

Baldspot stepped up onto the ledge around the outside of the tub, and stuck one toe into the water.

'See? It's not hot,' Bugeye said.

Baldspot carefully climbed in and sat on the ledge inside the tub with his chest sticking out of the water.

After a long soak, they got out, and soaped and scrubbed off the dead skin. Bugeye helped Baldspot first. He remembered how his father had once scrubbed his back for him with a rough cloth, and how he twisted away from his father's hands, complaining that it hurt, and how his father had given him a smack on the bum and told him not to exaggerate. As he shampooed Baldspot's hair, he saw that Baldspot had a burn scar on the back of his scalp. The patch of pale, wrinkled skin where the hair no longer grew was about the size of his palm. The hair at the top of Baldspot's head was so matted that it took several soapings, and when he rinsed it, the water ran black with grime.

Bugeye and Baldspot finished up in the bath, stepped out into the locker room, and saw themselves in the mirror: they looked like completely different children. Bugeye's naturally fair complexion had returned. His wet hair was ruffled, and his cheeks were flushed and vibrant. When they put on their new underwear and socks, and dressed themselves in their new clothes, they looked like two clever boys on their way home to a high-rise apartment having just finished up their after-school piano class or English class or what have you.

'I don't recognise you anymore, hyung,' Baldspot said with a laugh as they left the bathhouse.

'Me neither. No one would call you Baldspot now.'

'I do have a name. It's Yeong-gil.'

Bugeye stopped short and laughed with delight.

'Yeong-gil? That's been your name this whole time? Ha!'

'Hyung, what did they call you in school?'

To his own surprise, Bugeye found himself blurting out his old name.

'Jeong-ho. Choi Jeong-ho.'

Baldspot tittered. 'Choi Jeong-ho? Haha!'

As they walked, they kept calling each other by their names, bursting into laughter, and saying each other's names again. They caught another intercity bus across the river; as soon as they crossed the county line, they were in the outskirts of the city. Baldspot kept his head pressed to the window and stared in awe at the unfamiliar city passing by outside the window. Bugeye knew the area well: it was just a little further to where they could take the subway. Baldspot seemed overwhelmed by the unfamiliar sight of all the people on the street who looked and dressed nothing like the people of Flower Island. He turned to Bugeye.

'They look like the men in the management office.'

Bugeye was about to explain to Baldspot that, in this world, they were the ones who were different, but he caught himself. The bus reached its final stop on the outskirts of the city, and they got off and headed for the subway station. Baldspot looked terrified while riding the escalator.

'Hyung, where are we going? The stairs are moving.'

'We're going underground.'

'No! Let's go back up!'

'We're getting on the subway. It's a train that moves underground.'

In the subway car, Baldspot clung nervously to Bugeye's hand. Bugeye studied the subway map to figure out where they should get off; the first place he wanted to go was the intersection near the marketplace and his old neighbourhood, out on the eastern end of the city. It took close to an hour to get from one end of the city to the other. Baldspot fell asleep with his head on Bugeye's shoulder. Bugeye shook Baldspot awake and stepped out into the familiar-looking station. He walked fast, eager to get above ground.

'Hyung, I'm hungry.'

Bugeye realised from Baldspot's whining that they should have eaten right after they left the bathhouse. Once above ground, Bugeye spotted the pedestrian overpass and the familiar-looking shops near the intersection and the entrance to the market that was always clogged with motorcycles and small trucks. The boys headed for a Chinese restaurant on the second floor of a building near the corner of the entrance to the marketplace.

As they went up the stairs, Bugeye asked Baldspot, 'Have you had *jjajangmyeon* before?'

'No, what is it?'

Bugeye wordlessly pushed open the door to the restaurant with a practised hand. It was after lunchtime, but nearly all of the seats were full. They sat right next to the entrance, and Bugeye ordered two bowls of *jjajangmyeon* with a double serving of noodles. When the food came out, Baldspot's mouth split into a wide grin.

'I had this once a long time ago. I've been calling them black noodles.'

'Where did you live before?'

'Dunno. Can't remember. I went to school for a little while, and then my mum went away, and I moved to Flower Island with my dad.'

It had been so long since Bugeye had eaten *jjajangmyeon* that he could hardly slow down enough to chew the noodles, and kept swallowing them whole instead. Baldspot polished off the last of the black bean sauce in his bowl and said to Bugeye, 'Hyung, let's live here.'

'We can always come back. We'll bring Mum next time.'

Bugeye took his little brother into the chaos of the marketplace. He went back to the spot where his mother had sold her wares. At first, the other ladies there didn't recognise him, but when he crouched down and greeted them, one of the women gave a shout.

'*Aigu*, who is this? Aren't you the son of that nice lady?'

The cheerful woman who sold vegetables and was always ready with a smile was excited to see him.

'You look good!' she said with a hearty laugh. 'Did you mother remarry? Is your new neighbourhood treating you well?'

Bugeye couldn't resist the urge to brag, as they all did in that neighbourhood.

'Yes, my mum has her own store now.'

'And who's this?'

'My little brother.'

'So you got yourself a new daddy, huh?'

With all of the commotion that the women were making, Bugeye's original idea of visiting the girls in the sweatshop and the boys from his old neighbourhood went away. He had missed this place ever since moving to Flower Island, and yet now that he was here, the feeling faded. Bugeye stuck his hand in his pocket and ran his fingers over the still thick stack of bills. He led Baldspot out of the market.

'Where are we going now, hyung?'

Bugeye had one specific destination in mind. Once, back when his father was in charge of a small crew of junk collectors that manned one of the city districts, Bugeye and his parents had gone out to eat together. He remembered that they'd eaten *bulgogi* somewhere downtown, and that his father had said it was his mother's birthday. That day, his father had led them into a department store on the main street to buy Bugeye's mother a pair of shoes for her birthday; they'd wandered up and down and all around the different floors until they stumbled across an enormous display of toys. Children were crowded around near the staircase, so Bugeye ran over to see what they were looking at. A tiny train raced along a miniature track. There were tiny stations, and a forest and a village, tiny houses with pointed roofs, and miniature people no bigger than Bugeye's fingers. Off to the side, a bear lumbered, a rabbit hopped, a monkey beat a drum. As Bugeye begged his father to buy him the train, his father snatched him up off the floor and carried him downstairs. Bugeye never forgot about that busy street and the department store.

The two boys rode the bus thirty minutes to the southern end of the city centre. At a big intersection, Baldspot stared, his jaw hanging open, at all of the shiny office buildings and hotels and stores of every size, and at bars and restaurants, while Bugeye dragged him along by the hand in search of the department store. There were only a few days left until Christmas: strings of lights blinked from every tree along the road, and everywhere Christmas decorations glittered and sparkled.

Finally, Bugeye spotted a building with a giant Santa Claus dressed all in red and riding a sleigh driven by reindeer. The entire front of the building was plastered with decorations: gift boxes wrapped in red ribbons, fluffy white snow drifts, and individual snowflakes in every possible colour, magnified and sparkling like stars. The Christmas tree near the entrance was hung with gold and silver, and red and blue balls and cottony snowflakes, and at the very top shone a single enormous star. All around them was the bright, cheery sound of carols. Baldspot looked positively bewitched.

'Who's that old guy?'

Bugeye told Baldspot the same thing the grown-ups had told him when he was younger.

'That's Santa Claus. He goes around at night when everyone's asleep, and leaves presents for good girls and boys.'

Baldspot's face fell.

'I read about him in a picture book at the church school,' he said. 'But I don't think he ever visits our neighbourhood.'

Bugeye told him exactly what he'd been thinking ever since he was little.

'It's just a lie they made up so they can sell stuff.'

'Good thing we've got the Mr. Kims then,' Baldspot said with his usual giggle.

Bugeye thought about the fact that the *dokkaebi* would never, ever come to this street, and he inwardly felt happy about that. The entrance to the department store was crowded with women and children: it turned out there was a chocolate stand set up just in front. There was a big stack of everything—from boxed chocolates, to small packets of chocolate decorated in different colours, to individual chocolates wrapped in shiny red and blue-and-silver foil. A bowl was piled high with perfect little squares of chocolate, colourful chocolate balls shaped like bird eggs, chocolates with almonds embedded inside, and more. A young, uniformed woman was handing out exactly one piece each to the children crowded around her. Bugeye shoved his way up to the front of the bowl, plunged his hand in, and hurried away with a fistful of chocolate. The woman started to say something, her face showing her annoyance, but she just as quickly gave up.

Baldspot wolfed down the pieces of chocolate that Bugeye gave him and asked, 'Hyung, who makes this stuff? My tongue is melting.'

Bugeye took him by the hand and led him into the department store. The shiny glass and endless variety of objects in their display cases made them dizzy. The two boys swam through the crowd of people, heading past the sparkling displays of cosmetics and perfume and watches and necklaces and jewellery, to the escalator that never stopped moving up, up, up. At the next floor, they had to walk all the way around in a circle before they found the next up escalator. After stumbling through the first time, Bugeye swiftly caught his bearings, and at each floor he led them confidently around in a circle and up to the next.

Finally, he found what he was searching for. Dolls, stuffed animals, action figures. Cars, planes, tanks, helicopters. A train racing along its tracks just like the one he'd seen as a little boy. Toy handguns, machine guns, ray guns, and robots. Fire engines and police cars and race cars. Boxes filled with dozens of miniature automobiles. And video games. Of every variety. Bugeye's jaw hung open. Baldspot's hung even lower. All they could do was stand there frozen and stare in awe at the array of marvellous items that surrounded them. Finally, Baldspot came to and slowly made his way around the store, picking up the first toy he saw at every step, studying it, squeezing it, rolling it, and smiling nonstop. An employee in a button-down shirt and tie came over to Baldspot.

'See something you like, kid? Look but don't touch, okay?'

Bugeye looked up at the man and said boldly, 'I'm buying a present for my little brother.'

'That so? Hang on a sec. All the kids are going crazy over this.'

The employee took down a box from a shelf, and pulled out something the size of a small book. He pressed a button, and a light appeared: a figure on the screen began to move.

'I can see you've heard of it,' he said. 'It's called Super Mario.'

Baldspot's eyes were fixed on the tiny Mario in his red cap bouncing and flying and jumping walls and leaping across rivers and fighting off monsters. The employee pressed the buttons, demonstrating the game for them. The music and the sound effects—every *bo-yoing*, every *ka-ching*—made it seem all the more real. The employee handed the game to Baldspot, and the little guy sat right down on the floor, propped the game against his knees, and started pressing away at the buttons. His signature giggle soon had other customers in the shop glancing his way and laughing, too.

'It runs on batteries,' the employee explained. 'So you can play with it anywhere you go. Are you thinking of buying this for your brother? It's a little expensive.'

Bugeye kept his poker face, but he'd fallen for the game just as hard as Baldspot had. With the two of them taking turns, they could while away a whole day in an instant.

'I'll take one.'

'Of course. You boys are in luck. We're the only store that sells it.'

When Bugeye went up to the register, took out his cash, and started to count out the bills, the employee's eyes widened.

'Well, look at you, a regular tycoon! Did your mother give you all that money?'

'I withdrew it from my savings,' Bugeye said without looking up.

The employee handed him the receipt.

'Hold onto this. If you have any problems with it, you can bring it back for a repair or an exchange. Are you looking for anything else? Perhaps War of the Worlds? That might be up your alley ...'

Bugeye declined, and took the shopping bag with the new game inside. When he went back, Baldspot was still absorbed in the demo game.

'I bought us a new one.'

Baldspot put the game back on the shelf, ran after Bugeye, and snatched the shopping bag from his hands.

'I'll carry it.'

They headed back to the escalator. Each time they alighted on a lower floor, there were so many items on display, so much overwhelming variety, that they couldn't keep track of what they'd seen and what they hadn't yet seen. Bugeye stopped at a display of wool hats, gloves, and scarves. He'd been thinking about buying a pair of gloves and a scarf for his mother. As he browsed, he noticed a girl walking down one of the aisles in the store across the way. She looked the same as when he'd seen her on the overpass. The ends of her bobbed hair just brushed the tops of her shoulders, and she wore a chestnut-coloured coat and black socks.

Bugeye walked towards her in a trance. But when he turned the corner, she'd disappeared without a trace. Bugeye walked up and down the aisles looking for her before spotting her on an escalator heading up. He ran over to the escalator, but she had her back to him and was nearly to the top. Without a second thought, he ran up the escalator two steps at a time. When he got to the top, he saw her standing in a stationery store looking at something. He walked right over to her without pausing to catch his breath. But before he could approach her, he stopped dead. He couldn't remember what he was planning to say or do; his mind had gone completely blank. He couldn't say something stupid like, *Hey, don't I know you from somewhere, imagine running into each other like this, it's good to see you.* And he couldn't act like the older boys from his old neighbourhood and say, *Hey girl, can I get your number?* What did he think would happen when he came running after her like this? The female employee who'd been in the middle of explaining something to the girl stared at Bugeye. The girl glanced ever so slightly over her shoulder at him and turned back to the employee. Her face wasn't the one he had expected after all. She was just one of the countless unknown schoolgirls Bugeye could have passed on the street anywhere; the lustre that he thought he'd spotted from a distance wasn't actually there. Bugeye heaved a sigh of simultaneous disappointment and relief, and kept walking. He took a quick spin through the store and then headed back downstairs. How lucky for him that it wasn't the same girl. He sensed all too vividly how miserable he would've been if it had been her.

Too late, Bugeye realised that Baldspot was not by his side. He ran all around the floor in a panic, searching for Baldspot's sky-blue cap, but he could not find him. During his brief moment of distraction, Baldspot must have unknowingly kept going downstairs on his own, and was probably right at that moment searching for Bugeye. The thought filled Bugeye with worry. He took the elevator down another floor, searching the crowd as he went, and walked around every shop on that floor, but Baldspot was gone. He went all the way to the lowest floor, which was the most crowded of them all, walked around in a circle, and then headed back upstairs. He told himself that Baldspot had definitely been with him on the floor where gloves were sold, so he must not have looked hard enough.

He walked along the outer wall of the entire floor, searching all around, and crisscrossed each narrow, labyrinthine aisle that cut through the displays in the centre of the floor. Where had that brat gone? Now on the verge of tears, Bugeye headed back down again, retracing his steps over each floor. By the time he returned to the ground floor, Bugeye was worn out from worry and anger. He squatted down by a pillar when, from somewhere, a familiar wail met his ears. He sprang up and ran towards the sound. He spotted a blue cap surrounded by a ring of people. Baldspot was crying, and a tall young man in a necktie was holding their shopping bag. Bugeye grabbed Baldspot's hand.

'There you are!' he said. 'Why are you crying?'

'That man took my game. He says I stole it.'

Bugeye gave the man a menacing look.

'Where's your receipt?' the man demanded.

Bugeye deliberately pulled out his wad of cash along with the crumpled receipt from his jacket pocket.

'See,' he said, unfurling the receipt. 'I bought it for him.'

'Ah, so you did …'

The employee had probably spotted a little boy in

a cheap parka running with a shopping bag, and got suspicious. As Bugeye led Baldspot towards the exit, he turned and shouted at the employee loudly enough for everyone standing nearby to hear.

'Arsehole!'

As soon as they were outside, Bugeye felt dizzy and thirsty.

'Where the hell did you go?' he said to Baldspot.

'Hyung, you took off without saying anything! I thought you went downstairs without me, so I ran down to look for you.'

They went across the street and into a fast-food restaurant. They placed the hamburgers and French fries and sodas they'd ordered on a table facing the window, and gazed out at the parade of cars and people outside. As he ate, Baldspot's face was beaming again, as if he hadn't been bawling his eyes out just a moment ago.

'Hey, this is tasty. I wish I could eat this every day,' he said with a giggle.

'Is this the first time you've had a hamburger?'

Baldspot nodded. Bugeye felt like he was Baldspot's father; he imagined for a moment that his own father had brought them there. His eyes burned, and he turned his head and pretended to be looking around the inside of the restaurant. He spotted another group of girls. There were three of them, all dressed in school uniforms and chattering with each other. But for some reason he felt different from the way he had before, and merely gazed at them the way a grown-up might. He felt like he was watching a movie, and he could not enter the screen. Already the brief winter sun was setting, and dusk was falling over the city streets. The lights on the trees glittered even more brightly than in the day, and the displays in the shop windows floated like paintings in the dark.

6

New Year's passed, and the snow that had fallen all winter long finally stopped, giving way to better weather. The adults all talked about how the wind was no longer biting. When the snow fell, it buried the trash beneath it, making it much harder to sort out and collect items, and the ground could not be flattened back down and covered with fill dirt. The dirt that was spread quickly congealed with the snow and turned to sludge; the only alternative was to leave the exposed trash to freeze in place. Still, every day, more trash was poured on top of the old trash. As the weather warmed, the snow and ice below would melt and form air pockets, and cave-ins would happen with increasing frequency. The adults talked about bringing in backhoes to tamp down the trash. The rush of the New Year's holiday passed, and the trash pickers of Flower Island all waited for spring.

Before New Year's, Bugeye's mother was able to switch from the district sector to a private sector. The company was called Central Recycling, and those who paid the permit fee were assigned to a garbage truck and put in charge of that truck's work unit. Profits were split among the unit leaders and their teams. Each company president owned ten or twenty trucks, and took the items that the work units and their leaders collected to either recycle themselves in their own recycling plants or sold them to bigger factories. Everyone called them the Flower Island *chaebols*, the big CEOs of the trash world, and the districts their privately owned trucks collected from were the city's cream of the crop. Naturally, ownership of these districts was strictly guarded, so not just anyone could get access to those dumps. Bugeye's mother was a clever and determined woman who shrewdly managed the items that came from her assigned truck. She had a dozen people working under her. Rumour had it that when the Baron went to prison, he gave over half of the money in his account to her, and everyone agreed that it was the natural and logical thing to do.

That night, when Bugeye and Baldspot returned from their outing in the city, they told their mother about the money they'd found in the trash; she immediately pulled back the linoleum to see for herself. Bugeye added the remaining cash in his pocket to the hiding spot. His mother calmly announced that once the weather warmed up, they would rent themselves a room in the village across the stream and move out of the shantytown. From that point on, she renamed Baldspot 'Lucky.' She still sometimes called him Yeong-gil, but more often she would say, *Where's Lucky gone off to?* Though she didn't scold Bugeye for taking Baldspot with him and spending some of the cash, she declared herself in charge of the money from then on, and said they would use it sparingly. Otherwise, she pointed out, their neighbours might know something was up. For poor people, money that had been thrown away could rightfully belong to anyone. Bugeye and Baldspot, in turn, stuck to the vow they'd made to each other, and did not breathe a word of the Mr. Kim *dokkaebi* or Scrawny's house to their mother.

Now that the work was getting easier again, the only work Bugeye, Baldspot, and their mother had to do was sort and gather the items that her unit collected from the dumpsite. Their mother went to work by herself in the morning, and the boys joined her from afternoon to evening. Since moving to the private sector, Bugeye had been bumping into Mole more often while at work. Mole's job was to assist his older brother, who was a member of their father's private-sector work unit. Bugeye was transporting a sack filled with plastic bottles when Mole slunk over and sat near him.

'Hey, Bugeye, let's go into town today.'

'Why? What's up?'

'There's a movie I want to see.'

Bugeye feigned indifference.

'Been a long time since I even watched TV. What's so great about this movie?'

'It's called *Star Wars*. Supposed to be really good. The middle schoolers won't stop talking about it.'

'Hang on.'

Bugeye restacked the scrap metal and cardboard, covered it with a tarp, and stood up. Then he ran home, changed his shirt, and rejoined Mole. They crossed the bridge over the stream and caught the next bus into town. A middle-aged man who looked like he'd had a little too much to drink yelled at them.

'Hey, why can't you Flower Island jerks get your own bus? Stop stinking up ours!'

Undaunted, Mole hollered right back, 'Fuck off, you old prick!'

The man was stunned to find himself confronted by such a young punk, and muttered under his breath for a moment before falling silent. They got off at the town bus stop and walked over to the main street.

'I'll get the tickets if you pay for dinner,' Mole said.

'What do you want? There's a place in the market that serves blood-sausage soup.'

Mole immediately nodded. 'They say pork fat is the best thing to eat after you've been breathing in a lot of dirt.'

'Says who?'

'My older brother, for one. Sometimes he boils a whole hunk of pork, and eats it with a bottle of soju.'

They headed first to the blood-sausage soup restaurant and got a seat in the corner. There were no other dinner customers; the only people there were three elderly folk who looked like they worked in the marketplace. They were drinking soju and eating slices of boiled pig's head. When the woman who ran the restaurant came to their table, Bugeye ordered two bowls of blood-sausage soup.

'And a bottle of soju,' Mole added.

'What?' the woman said. 'Nothing doing. You two are underage.'

One of the men at the other table glanced over in his drunken haze and butted in.

'Aw, go ahead and give it to them. We won't tell anyone. How old are you two?'

Mole shrunk his head down into his shoulders like a turtle and muttered, 'Eighteen.'

'Hell, that's old enough to enlist in the army. When I was in middle school, we used to get drunk off our rockers on makkolli.'

Bugeye and Mole silently ate their soup. After they'd spooned up every last drop, they headed back out as Bugeye grumbled.

'Dumbarse, why'd you have to say we're eighteen? So embarrassing ... Look, do you really want soju?'

'When I saw what they were having in there, I just wanted a taste.'

At the first hole-in-the-wall shop they came across,

Bugeye ran inside and came out with a bottle of soju. He handed it to Mole.

'A little something for the movie.'

Inside the theatre were only a handful of kids and their parents; nearly all of the seats in front were empty. Bugeye and Mole stuck their feet up on the backs of the seats in front of them and sprawled out. While the hero of the movie travelled through outer space and defeated imperial robots with a light sabre, Mole and Bugeye passed the soju bottle, concealed in its black plastic bag, back and forth. Their stomachs grew warm, and their cheeks flushed. Bugeye had gotten drunk once before on makkolli that the women in the market alleyways gave him as a joke, but this was his first taste of soju. He was guessing that Mole had drunk it before. After each big swig, Mole let out a throaty *kyaaa*, as if he knew his way around a bottle. By the time they emptied the bottle, the alcohol was hitting them hard.

'I feel really warm.'

'My head is pounding.'

They kept cackling and punching each other on the shoulders, not hiding how drunk they were. The hero piloted a fighter plane and fired a missile at a weak spot on the empire's huge, ball-like space station, and the screen filled with flames as the movie drew to a close. Bugeye and Mole left the theatre and boarded a bus, limp of limb but still high of spirit.

'I dunno why I'm not getting any taller. I go to bed each night and wake up every morning, but I'm still just a little kid,' Mole grumbled.

Bugeye thought about how the older boys back home used to cause trouble the moment they started growing pubic hair, and how the ones who left the neighbourhood or stopped showing their faces around town once they turned nineteen would pretend not to know the younger boys on the rare occasion that they did bump into each other. Bugeye had already wised onto the fact that becoming a grown-up did not mean good things were waiting for you. He and Mole crossed back over the stream, and were on their way to the dumpsite when they saw the red flashing lights of an ambulance and a crowd of people in front of the management office. A familiar-looking picker from one of the private sectors spotted Mole in the crowd.

'Hurry! Your brother got hurt!'

'My hyung?'

Mole squeezed through the crowd and ran toward the ambulance. Bugeye followed on his heels. Mole's father was standing in front of the ambulance; Mole's brother had already been loaded inside. Mole called out to his brother and jumped into the back while his father explained to someone dressed in a white coat that they were family. Before the paramedic closed the back door, he said, 'We can only take one person.'

The door shut and the ambulance took off, siren

wailing. It turned out that as the last truck of the day was dumping its load, the ground beneath it had caved in, and the truck had tipped—right onto Mole's older brother as he was guiding the driver.

'We have to be careful now that it's spring. The whole place is covered in layers of coal ash and ice, so there are air pockets everywhere.'

'Why haven't those arseholes brought in the heavy equipment yet? They need to tamp down the ground.'

'Tell me about it. There's so much gas escaping from underneath the trash now that I can barely breathe when I'm working.'

Everyone was chattering loudly. Bugeye asked one of the older unit members if he knew what had happened. The man said he saw everything.

'Betcha he loses his legs. He was trapped under there for a good twenty minutes. The only equipment we had was a bulldozer and an excavator, so we were barely able to push the truck off him.' He lowered his voice and added, 'When we pulled him out, his legs were shredded.'

Bugeye joined the dispersing crowd and headed back to the shantytown. When he got home, the light was on in his mother's room, and he could hear a series of electronic pings and trills coming from his and Baldspot's room. He stuck his head into his mother's room first.

'There was an accident … Someone was crushed by one of the Co-op trucks.'

'I heard. We all have to be careful. You eat?'

'I did.'

He closed the door, afraid to talk too long for fear that she'd smell the alcohol on his breath. When he went into his own room, Baldspot was lying on his stomach with a pillow under his chest, completely absorbed in playing Super Mario Bros. He'd gotten so good at it that he'd passed nearly all of the obstacles and difficult parts, and was nearing the final castle. His goal lately had been to reach the last spot where he would be greeted with fireworks and fanfare. Bugeye lay down next to him and watched him play.

'Hey, hey,' he said, 'There's a sewer pipe. If you go inside, you'll find a secret world.'

'I know ...' Baldspot started to say, but then he rolled away and shouted, 'Ew, you stink! Hyung, were you drinking?'

'Shut up. Mum'll hear.'

While Baldspot was distracted, Mario was killed by some kind of lizard monster, and fell down a cliff.

'You made me die!' Baldspot said, finally putting the game down.

'Have you been to Scrawny's house lately?'

'Yeah, Scrawny's mama is sick. She's not talking.'

Over New Year's, Bugeye had gone with Baldspot to Scrawny's house for a holiday meal of rice-cake soup, and after dark had briefly seen the Mr. Kim *dokkaebi* down by the bend in the stream. But ever since his mother had changed sectors, Bugeye had taken to going into town whenever he had free time, and had all but stopped dropping by to see Peddler Grandpa.

'What about the child?'

'The Mr. Kims are busy now that spring is coming. They say the bad fog is spreading over more of their village.'

'Their village … Was it really there? Did we just dream it all?'

Bugeye was still doubtful, but Baldspot giggled and said, 'I dreamed about that department store you took me to.'

A few days later, Bugeye had finished work and was heading home when he saw Mole stumbling along the path ahead of him. A group of women standing in front of a shack whispered amongst themselves and stepped out of his way. Bugeye passed his own shack and kept going, keeping a careful distance as he followed Mole. Just as he suspected, Mole left the shantytown and staggered up the hill. When Bugeye hurried to catch up to him, Mole turned and threw his arm around Bugeye's shoulder.

'Well, look who it is, my pal Bugeye.'

'Man, why do you drink so much?'

'Fuck you, man. I found a bottle of whiskey at work, and had a few drinks. So what.'

He pulled something wrapped in a black plastic bag out of the pocket of his coveralls, and held it aloft.

'And here's another bottle of soju.'

Bugeye helped Mole stagger down the other side of the hill, and headed for the hideout. They lit a candle and sat down across from each other with the blanket and sleeping bag on their laps. Mole cracked open the bottle of soju with his teeth and started to gulp it down; Bugeye had to pry the bottle away from him. Mole's lips curled, and he burst into tears.

'My hyung, they cut off both his legs. He'll never walk again. And all our old man can talk about is getting compensated.'

'You've had enough to drink. I'll have the rest.'

Bugeye remembered how well he'd slept after his first taste of alcohol a few days earlier, so he thought he could handle soju just fine. Plus, the feeling of sudden adulthood that came with getting drunk wasn't bad either. But unlike before, he'd had nothing to eat, and the cold soju made the inside of his stomach tingle. After a few more swallows, his face and body grew hot, and the soju began to taste sweet. They sat together for an hour, Mole insisting that he was going to drink more, and Bugeye insisting that he better not.

Mole stopped sniffling and took something that looked like a tube of toothpaste out of his pocket. He squirted the contents into a plastic bag, held it open, and brought it up to his face. Bugeye knew all too well what he was doing, but he didn't bother to stop him. He'd tried it once himself back in his old neighbourhood. All of the kids, from the older boys to the boys his age to the little guys, had sat in a circle in an abandoned house slated for demolition, and took sniffs of the glue inside before passing the bag to the next kid. Some threw up; some writhed around, unable to catch their breath; some went limp, like they were dead, only to suddenly stagger to their feet and totter around. Mole took several deep breaths and fell over on his back. After a while, he got up, unsteady on his feet.

'Heh, your face is all stretched out.' He pointed at Bugeye and laughed.

Bugeye slipped the plastic bag Mole had dropped into his pocket. Mole flapped his arms and pretended to fly.

'I'm soaring, man. Totally soaring.'

Mole caught his knee on the low table and fell over, snuffing out the candle as he went. When Bugeye sat him back up, he started groping around on the floor.

'Hey,' Bugeye said, 'let's go home. Come on.'

'Where's it? Gotta huff some more.'

Bugeye forced Mole to his feet and walked him out of the hideout. They climbed the hill much more slowly than before, stopping to rest partway, then climbing a little more, then stopping to rest again. They crossed the field, fording their way through the tall, dried grass. Bugeye kept his arm around Mole, whose arms and legs kept flailing around like an octopus. They came to a clearing where Hard Hat was having drinks with his work crew.

'Ha! Look at these brats,' said Hard Hat. 'Still wet behind the ears, and already they're out getting drunk and acting crazy.'

Bugeye was exhausted, so he let go of Mole for a moment to catch his breath.

'His brother lost both his legs,' he told the men.

Bugeye said nothing more, but the men understood at once.

'Drinking will only make it worse.'

'Do you know where he lives?'

'He lives in the place across from mine,' said one of the men, who wore a knit cap. 'His dad sleeps somewhere else.'

The man in the cap stepped forward and hoisted Mole easily onto his back, then took off down the road to the shantytown. When Bugeye got home, the shack was empty; Baldspot had left again. The alcohol hit him all at once. Bugeye sat with his back against the wall and muttered to himself, *Great job, pounding all that goddamn alcohol, gonna rot here, just like the Baron, or Mole's brother, or Mole.* As Bugeye sprawled out on the blanket, a thought occurred to him and he reached into his pocket. The plastic bag crinkled, and he hesitated for only a second before grabbing it with both hands, spreading it open, and placing the bag over his nose and mouth. *Whatever,* he thought, *who gives a shit?* He inhaled deeply, the smell of rubber and petrol filling his nose and throat, and then his head was spinning and he couldn't breathe. He pulled the bag away from his face and then brought it up for another inhale. The inside of his head droned with the sound of cicadas at the height of summer, and everything started to go black. He groped around on the floor for somewhere to rest his head, his arms flailing. His hand fell on something. What was it? He fumbled with the object for a bit before accidentally hitting one of the buttons. The screen lit up.

Electronic music fills my ears. The screen grows bigger, and bigger, and with a brrr, my body shrinks down. I am dressed in blue overalls and a red cap, and I am walking straight ahead. To each side of me are walls made from fake stone blocks and directly ahead is a door. The moment I walk through the door, a new world appears. The sky is a bright blue, and big round clouds float by. To one side is a jagged forest. If I look hard, off in the distance I can see the flat line where bright blue sky meets dark yellow earth. When I look closer, the blue of the sky is paint, and the clouds are clumps of urethane foam, and the forest is plastic and vinyl, and the earth is latex and rubber pellets pounded flat, and the grass is polypropylene, and the side of the road and the walls and the fake rocks are synthetic plastic. Cement buildings sparkling with metal and glass stand like scattered towers in a vast plain. It looks like a brand-new city that has just recently been built. But there are no other people besides me. Grape vines and apple trees grow along the edge of a flowerbed where the leaves have unfurled and the plastic flowers are in full bloom, and the grapes and apples are smooth, shiny plastic.

Up ahead, something, some sort of shaggy dog, is coming towards me. Its polyester fur sticks out in all directions, and its eyes are red and it is growling. I keep walking. I figure this creature will move aside for me, but, oh no! The moment I touch it, a jolt of electricity runs through my body and I flash through a screen that reminds me of a window filled with very bright light, and I plummet into darkness. Light breaks again, and I am back on the narrow path between the brick walls, back where I started, and I pass through the door. I walk the same path as before, past the flowerbed, and here comes the dog creature. This time I turn around and go back the way I came, but there is another one. This one looks like a tortoise; it crawls with its belly pressed to the ground. They are on both sides of me and coming closer. I push off with my feet a little and, boom, my body is aloft. I push a little harder and I'm bouncing high into the sky. I bounce and land on the tortoise creature: with a bloop-bloop it pops like a bubble and vanishes. I bounce again and land on the dog creature, and there's another bloop-bloop. This time, a line of creatures marches towards me. I bounce, bounce, bounce, and pop each one in *turn. Floating in the sky are stones, staggered like a staircase. I bounce, bounce again, and at the very top I bump into a small star; I grow in power, and the score I accumulate appears in sparkling gold numbers in the sky. I leap onto an embankment across the way and cross a log bridge. Ahead are the dog creatures; in the sky are bats looking like scraps of tissue. I bounce on the heads of the dog creatures, kick the bat creatures out of the sky, one-two, one-two, bloop-bloop, and cross another bridge.*

I cannot turn back now. I cannot speed up either, can only march along in step with the solemn music. Oops! I don't make it across an open manhole, and down I go. I fall through darkness, and enter a cave-like underground world. The scenery is completely changed. A river of sticky paint flows past; fake rocks and an acrylic waterfall tumble down. Everywhere I turn is crawling with rubber balloon creatures shaped like tiny, horned crocodiles. They reek of petrol. I jump on them, too, and pop them. An enormous mountain of trash looms before me. There's a bog of sticky black grease, a pond that shoots out flames, a tangle of junk—some like cans, some like long bottles, some like crumpled rags, some like twisted balls of wire, some like broken boxes—and a long rope hangs down from the very top. I grab the rope and rise. Up there, an even bigger crocodile spreads its jaws. I bounce and fly through the air, kick him with both feet, and vanquish him.

I cross the bridge: there stands the king of the underworld in his fluttering cloak. Fire spews from his mouth. If the fire touches me, I'll have to tumble back down into darkness. I bound up stepping stones floating in thin air and alight at a higher place. Then I soar down and kick the monster in the head, once, twice, three times, kwang-kwang-kwang, and he explodes, and with the last of my strength, I swoop over and claim the golden bead glittering atop a plate. The music swells, fireworks explode, and my score, my winnings, sparkle in the sky. Just above the still-exploding fireworks, an opening gapes. I flap hard to reach it, and at last I emerge from the dark and gloomy cave and into a different landscape. It's the same open field from before. Here, I can speak to no one, see no one, receive help from no one. The houses, trees, rocks, and rivers are all obstacles, and the monsters intent on sending me back to the beginning are my enemy. I cannot turn back, all I can do is move endlessly forward, and skip and soar and grasp and hang and push, all while raising my score. I barely make it past the first stage, and then I am back, standing before a door that leads into a high castle. The path I have travelled has been pushed off the edge of the screen and there is no way back, no retreat. It is an endlessly

*repeating parade, and even if I reach the highest stage,
I return as always to where I started.*

*I stand before the castle door when I hear a raspy
voice behind me. Child, do not go. I want to trust
the voice, but surely it's a trap. I turn and look:
Grandfather Kim is standing there. What are you
doing here? I ask, and he says, Everyone who goes
down that road meets their ruin. They think it's a
shortcut, but they pay a terrible price. Do not forget
that every living thing and every object in this world is
connected to you. Just then, a memory, like a longed-
for dream, comes back to me and I call out, I've been
to your village, is it different from here? Of course it's
different, he says. But our village is always with you.
We're here because you're here, and when you vanish,
we vanish. We live with you and are the same as you,
down to every last tree, every blade of grass, every duck,
every mountain, every river. Here, everything is an
obstacle and you are alone, surrounded by monsters
that you must fight and destroy. Can't you see that
this path will keep you running forever, bent only
on making it to the next stage? You don't have to go
through that door. You can leave this place.*

Wait, did he just shove me?

The horrible landscape vanished at once. Just like that,
Bugeye was back in a candlelit room, lying on his side with

his legs curled to his chest and his arms wrapped around his head. He thought he was still falling and falling.

'Hyung! What's wrong?'

Baldspot was standing there with the game in his hand. Bugeye struggled to speak.

'W–water ...'

His tongue was so dry that he could barely get the words out. Baldspot held a bowl of water up to his mouth, and Bugeye took a long drink. The water wet the thick cardboard of his tongue and poured down his feverish throat. A surge of helpless regret washed over him, and with a curse, he closed his eyes.

*

That day, the sky was very overcast, and the wind blew hard. The banner in front of the management office declaring spring as the season of safety awareness was tattered and torn, and all but flying away on the wind. The evening's line of garbage trucks had started crowding in around five, and the final shift was in full swing. The days were now longer than in winter, and a red glow still lingered in the western sky, while all around, the air was growing dusky. Bugeye's mother began collecting items from her unit. Bugeye and Baldspot worked together to separate the items in the baskets that the workers ferried over to them, stuff them into large sacks, and gather them all in one place. Someone on her unit began to complain.

'The Environmental Co-operative is going too far! They've left us barely enough room for our trucks to turn around.'

'The unit leaders for Central Recycling spoke to them yesterday,' Bugeye's mother said. 'The Co-op said they would fix it.'

Another worker dumped their load and said, 'Fix it? Shit … Look over there. They dumped those oil drums yesterday, but the drums are still sticking out. The backhoes only went over one area, and everything else they dumped today is just sitting there.'

'The stuff we're getting is useless—there aren't enough items worth collecting. This area is meant for household waste only. They should be disposing of those oil drums somewhere else … The Co-op must have taken a bribe.'

'I get your point. If they don't take care of it by tomorrow, I'll talk it over with the other unit leaders and go to the Co-op again.'

Bugeye's mother tried to console her team before heading over to their work site. As the trash built up, the space they had to work in had narrowed, but it was still big enough for the trucks to squeeze through. Even so, her unit members' complaints weren't unfounded. Out of all of the available space, the Environmental Co-operative had picked a spot right in the middle of the entrance to dig a deep pit, and had been burying useless materials in it over the past few days. They said it was because the heavy-equipment operators would demand more money if they were asked to cover a wider area.

Nevertheless, the day had passed without any particular trouble until just past six o'clock, when a loud blast was heard coming from the district sector over to the east, and flames were seen shooting up. As the layers of trash buried underground rotted, the air pockets had filled with gas; with the warming weather, the ice was melting as well, and the gas was finding its way out. The wind fanned the flames, and the fire began to sputter and spread in all directions. Luckily, the district workers had finished their shift and were just that moment making their way down from the dumpsite, so no one was burned or injured, but they could not leave it be either. A call was made from the management office, and one fire truck from town and two from the city came running. It took half an hour to extinguish the flames. But that was only the beginning.

Bugeye and Baldspot arrived home first. Their mother didn't return until around 8.00 p.m., as she'd been busy finishing up for the day and holding a meeting with her work unit. Just like every other night, the three of them were eating dinner at the table together when there was a whooshing sound, followed by another loud blast. Their plastic door lit up. Bugeye and Baldspot went outside to discover flames rising up from the middle of the shantytown. Fireballs launched from the exploding gas in the landfill were raining down on roofs like cannon shells. The shantytown began to burn.

'Mum! Fire!'

Bugeye's mother glanced outside and hurriedly grabbed three blankets, shoving one each into Bugeye and Baldspot's hands, and took off towards the shop. The sky around the landfill was as bright as day: the whole area had turned into a sea of fire, and clouds of white gas billowed up. Everyone quickly regretted leaving their shacks without their cloth masks and gas masks and other equipment. The sound of explosions was constant, and sparks flew through the air before pouring down like hail. Bugeye's mother took the lead, her blanket covering her head as she ran bent forward at the waist, looking only straight ahead. Bugeye covered his head as well, and held his breath as he ran with his eyes fixed on the ground. The air around them smelled foul, and the sky was covered in a thick cloud of fumes. Baldspot had been following them, but he stopped in his tracks and looked back. He covered his head with his blanket and took off running in the opposite direction of Bugeye and his mother. He had to get back home and save that game. As the flames rose on all sides, Baldspot vanished into the dense smoke.

Bugeye and his mother ran towards the office, trying to get as fast and as far away as they could from the dumpsite. Countless people were pouring out of the shantytown; most were barefoot and empty-handed. The fire was spreading. Already all of the shacks had gone up in flames. The instant a single lick of flame touched them, those jerry-built structures made from vinyl and canvas and Styrofoam and cardboard and wooden boards caught fire like dry kindling; the walls bulged with heat, and collapsed in on themselves. The methane gas escaping the trash and the layers of flammable materials kept setting each other off, burning everything through and through, and as the heated air pockets exploded, more clouds of gas billowed out, until the flames reached the Co-op's carelessly discarded drums. There was an enormous explosion, and the drums became airborne. Some were later found floating in the middle of the river; others, crushed and dented on the edges of Flower Island. Sparks rained, gas billowed, and people collapsed in abandonment, unsure of which way to run, while others headed straight for the management office and church for the safety of their intact tin roofs. Two thousand shacks burned at once, and though the fire waned before long, the heat and the gas were worse than what was happening in the landfill. An employee of the management office shouted through a megaphone at the people crowding in.

'Please make your way across the river! You cannot stay here. It is too dangerous. You must evacuate!'

Bugeye and his mother lost each other in the smoke, and stumbled around searching and calling out for each other. Nearly everyone crowded around the management office was in the same state of panic, which made it even harder to find anyone. They floundered about, coughing, tears streaming.

'Jeong-ho! Yeong-gil!'

Bugeye heard his mother's voice, and spotted a familiar-looking blanket. Mother and son embraced as if meeting on a battleground.

'Where's your little brother?'

'I don't know.' Bugeye searched around. 'Maybe he went to Scrawny's house?'

Bugeye pushed his mother ahead of him, past the shop, out towards the open field. They headed for Scrawny's house on the western end of the island. The fire had spread from the landfill and the shantytown, and was burning the field that Bugeye and Baldspot usually crossed to get to their hideout. The flames were being swept along by the wind. They hurried along the smoky path towards Scrawny's house. They could hear the dogs barking excitedly in the distance.

'Where are we?' his mother asked nervously.

'This is where Peddler Grandpa lives.'

'I heard he lived nearby. So strange. It's like a different world out here.'

Peddler Grandpa must have already been pacing around outside, because he met them along the path.

'Who's there?' he called out.

Bugeye and his mother greeted him.

'What's going on?' he said. 'We've had fires before, but never like this.'

'Is Scrawny's mama feeling better?' Bugeye asked.

Peddler Grandpa dropped his voice to a whisper.

'She's sleeping like the dead right now. I'm worried she'll run off again if she finds out the island is on fire.'

He looked around.

'Where's your little brother?'

'We left the house together, but we lost him. I thought he'd be here ...'

'Let's wait and see. He'll come here when he can't find you.'

They sat in front of the house and watched the fire grow. Flames were licking the sides of the hill and torching the silver grass along the river's edge.

'Let's go inside, ma'am,' Peddler Grandpa said to Bugeye's mother.

'I don't want to impose.'

'We have an extra room. The three of you can sleep there.'

They tried to sneak in quietly, but there was no stopping the dogs from barking and whimpering. Bugeye picked up Scrawny, and the rest of the dogs quieted down. When they sat down, they heard Scrawny's mama's sleepy-sounding voice.

'Dad, is someone here?'

'No, go back to bed.'

They heard sirens off in the distance. The fire trucks had arrived too late. The trucks that had been dispatched earlier in the evening must have returned, along with reinforcements from the city. Bugeye's mother looked up from her seat in the corner and said to Bugeye, 'Go out and find your little brother.'

He'd been planning to look for him anyway. He headed towards the management office, the stream to his left, and the hill, field, and river to his right. The dry grass and trees in the field and on the hill were smouldering, and clouds of smoke billowed in the hazy sky above the burned-out shantytown, while flames were still climbing the landfill. Police cars were parked close together in front of the management office with its cloudbank of toxic smoke, and fire trucks were parked close to the trash. The crew leaders from the district and the unit leaders from the private sectors clustered together, armed with masks and gloves and work equipment. As Bugeye squeezed past them, one of them called out, 'Hey! Why haven't you evacuated yet?'

Bugeye took a closer look. It was Hard Hat. He called back, 'Have you seen my little brother?'

'All the kids left the island already. Where's your mum?'

'At Peddler Grandpa's house.'

Hard Hat gave Bugeye a firm shove on the back to send him on his way.

'You guys should be safe there, since it's out of the way.

Pretty much everyone else evacuated across the stream.'

Bugeye returned to Scrawny's house, figuring that Baldspot must have followed the crowd to the village. Despite still feeling jittery, Bugeye and his mother fell asleep in the spare room. Sometime in the middle of the night, Bugeye awoke. The dogs inside the house and the dogs outside in the greenhouse were barking. The windows were bright, as if a light had been turned on outside. Bugeye heard the front door bang open, and sensed someone running out of the house. When he went to look, the front door was wide open, and Scrawny was out in the front yard, yapping, while the other disabled dogs were on the porch and barking along with her. A dark-red light filled the sky. Bugeye's mother rushed out of the room, followed by Peddler Grandpa, who turned on the light and looked around, his eyes still bleary with sleep.

'That damn girl ran off again ...' he muttered.

He stuffed his feet into his shoes and ran out, Bugeye right on his tail. As soon as they hit the front yard, they saw why the dogs were barking so ferociously. The fire seemed to be moving up the bend in the stream. All at once, the thick silver grass went up in flames. The fire had made its way to them while they were asleep. Peddler Grandpa picked up Scrawny and put her on the porch and told Bugeye's mother, 'Stay in the house and shut the door.'

He ran towards the river. Bugeye followed. When they passed the pile of dismantled electronics, the flames were already getting close. Just ahead was a patch of silver grass taller than their heads; the entire field was covered in grass and weeds that'd had the entire winter to dry out. Peddler Grandpa dove into the tall grass.

'Stay there!' he yelled back at Bugeye.

He took off his shirt, wrapped it around his head, and disappeared into the woods near the river. Bugeye watched fearfully as the swiftly spreading flames came closer, walking backwards to keep his distance from them. After a moment, Peddler Grandpa emerged from the cloud of smoke billowing from the now-burning silver grass. He was carrying Scrawny's mama on his back. Her body was limp. He staggered back to the house and collapsed with her in the front yard.

'Wake up, child,' he said, gently patting her cheek. He turned to Bugeye. 'Go get some water.'

When Bugeye came back with a bowl of water, Scrawny's mama was on her feet, and Grandpa had his arms around her waist, trying to stop her from running off again. She flailed her arms and yelled.

'You bastards! You think you're the only ones who live here? Every last one of you bastards could disappear, and the world would still be here!'

'Okay, child. Okay. It's all my fault.'

Peddler Grandpa pressed her back down to a sitting position. He was exhausted and gasping for air. Bugeye tried to help by wrapping his arms around Scrawny's mama's waist. She tried to shake off their hands, and started yelling again.

'You think you're the only ones who live in this world?!'

The dogs, in both the house and the greenhouse, all barked in chorus at the sound of her voice. She tried a few more times to shake off Bugeye and Peddler Grandpa, but her spent body went limp again.

Flower Island burned for the next five days. The flames refused to die down, and the smoke and the fumes were carried on the wind over to the western end of the city that had sent all of its trash there in the first place, and further still, into the heart of the city. The river that cut through the middle of the city served as a conduit for the smoke, which quickly spread across the entire city. Hospitals and residential neighbourhoods were in an uproar to evacuate. Employees in the city's office buildings complained of headaches. As the fire spread, ten more fire trucks were sent to the island the next day, but there was so much ground to cover and so many chemicals that spraying water did little to extinguish it. It wasn't until the fourth day that the trash pickers, who'd gotten themselves sorted out, joined forces with sanitation workers from each district to put out the fire by loading up cultivators with fill dirt to spread onto the flames and by bringing in bulldozers to turn over the smouldering trash.

Baldspot's body was discovered two days later when

the flames and the smoke had subsided. In the process of clearing the fire damage and the remaining embers from the shantytown, the trash pickers found a dozen or more bodies—grown-ups and children alike. Baldspot had fallen with his blanket over his head and both feet poking out from beneath the scorched hem. Bugeye ran over to check, but the little guy's body was unburned. It looked like he'd been asphyxiated by the smoke. Bugeye watched as his mother, for the first time in years, wept openly, and loudly, in front of other people. There were other bodies, as well, already halfway reduced to ash. The surviving families were poor, and so they took the management office's advice and had the bodies of their loved ones cremated; the family members who returned with handfuls of ash went down to the river or out to the fields to scatter the remains. Bugeye picked up Baldspot's torn and restitched black baseball cap—the same old beat-up cap that Baldspot had refused to throw away and insisted on wearing everywhere he went, even after Bugeye bought him a brand-new sky-blue one.

Trash came out of each of the city's districts every day, but the trash pickers had lost their homes, and having lost all of the recyclables that they'd collected, they had no means of building new shacks. There were also many burn victims, and though the rest of the survivors looked okay on the outside, at least half of the pickers were suffering from the after effects. No one had been able to save anything from the fire; though, with time, they would be able to fish out other useful items from the trash and refurnish their lives once more.

Bugeye's mother said nothing, but he knew that the money they'd buried beneath the linoleum had burned up. The heat was so great that all of the Styrofoam and vinyl had melted together into one dark lump. And yet the garbage trucks kept marching in, day after day. Dozens upon dozens of temporary tents were pitched, and work resumed. Bugeye's mother took medication twice a day now and endured, while the rest of the trash pickers offered each other pills for their headaches.

Bugeye finished his afternoon shift, climbed the black ash-covered hill, and headed alone towards the hideout. All that was left in the ruins of the fire were the scorched cinder-block walls. The roof had burned and caved in, and the magazines and plastic toys and the table and the sleeping bag that they'd stashed inside had all blackened and melted into distorted shapes. Bugeye walked through the field where the shrubs and silver grass had been reduced to stumps and ash, and headed west towards Scrawny's house. Peddler Grandpa came out to the yard and watched as Bugeye made his way over.

'I heard about the kid. Poor thing ...' Peddler Grandpa said, patting Bugeye on the arm. Bugeye suppressed the pain in his throat and looked away. They stood there in silence for a moment.

'They say the city's planning to build some prefab homes for all of you.'

Bugeye looked over at Scrawny's house.

'I like it here,' he said.

'We've got the extra room. You two could move in.'

Bugeye peeked through the window and asked, 'Where's Scrawny's mama?'

Peddler Grandpa looked down at the ground.

'Probably asleep in her room,' he muttered. 'She hasn't eaten in days. Only drinks water. I'm afraid it might be time to send her to the hospital.'

Peddler Grandpa reached out and gave Bugeye's hand a squeeze.

'Guess those items you gave me will come in handy now,' he added.

They heard someone humming a slow melody, and when they turned to look, Scrawny's mama had come out of the house. They couldn't tell if it was the folk song 'Arirang' or that old ballad from the 1930s, 'Tears of Mokpo,' but when they listened closer, they realised she was talking to the tune of a song.

What to do, what to do? Can't live, can't die.
What to do, my poor babies? Can't stay, can't go.

She bobbed and swayed across the yard, her feet never seeming to touch the ground. Peddler Grandpa stuck a cigarette in his mouth and stood off to one side and watched, as if there were no point anymore in trying to stop her. Bugeye did what he'd once seen Baldspot do, and trailed politely after her. When Scrawny's mama turned and headed towards the bend in the stream, Peddler Grandpa walked over to Bugeye and stayed him by the arm.

'Don't go. You might run into trouble.'

'It's okay. I'll be fine.'

Bugeye walked slowly behind Scrawny's mama, whose limbs were limp and swaying like laundry hanging from a line. They walked through the ankle-deep ash where the silver grass had burned. When they got to the yard in front of the now-empty shrine, the pillars were all scorched, the roof was even uglier and more crooked than before, and nearly half of the tiles had fallen off and were lying in shards on the ground. The old willow tree that had stood in a once-lush stand of silver grass was burned black from roots to branches. Scrawny's mama ran her hands down the trunk and mumbled:

What to do, what to do? Can't live, can't die.
What to do, my poor babies? Can't stay, can't go.

She knelt down and swept her hands over the dirt at the base of the tree. The ash from the burnt grass billowed up and turned her hands and skirt black. She ran her hands down her face, turning her skin black. Then she looked around and walked over to the front of the yard where scorched branches stuck out of the ground. Bugeye followed her. The dense silver grass had all burned, leaving only black ash and a wide-open space. At the centre was a basin carved from stone that had once been fed by a spring; the water had long since dried up, and only little piles of sand and chipped stone remained.

Scrawny's mama stood in front of it, staring down at something. Bugeye went over to her and looked inside. There were items in the basin, all in a neat row, as if someone had placed them there. With a sudden burst of energy, Scrawny's mama stepped into the dry spring, picked up the items, and started chucking them at Bugeye's feet. A cracked wooden pestle. A cornstalk broom with the tips worn down. Two rubber shoes missing their heels, one belonging to a man and the other to a woman. A tarnished silver hairpin. Half of a water buffalo horn button from a traditional men's overcoat. A broken pipe. A bamboo comb missing its teeth. A frayed cloth thimble. A sleek axe handle carved from oak. A wooden spool with the lacquer flaking off. A half-burnt poker. A chipped rice scoop. A tiny wooden top. Some had been merely scorched, some half burned away, and some entirely untouched by the flames. Scrawny's mama stepped out of the spring and raked the items together without a word, and then picked up as much as she could carry and walked back to the shrine, while Bugeye, who had no idea what she was up to, picked up what he could carry and followed her. There were so many things that Bugeye had to make a second trip for the rest. Scrawny's mama peered under the raised floor of the shrine, which was scorched but otherwise intact.

'Stay with us,' she said. 'Don't go. Don't leave us.'

Scrawny's mama shoved each of the items they'd carried as far under the shrine as she could; Bugeye piled the items together, and handed them to her one by one. She carefully placed them side by side so they wouldn't overlap. The way she moved her hands made it look like she was laying each item down to rest and tucking it into bed.

While Scrawny's mama was absorbed in her task, Bugeye blurted out, 'Why are you treating these useless things like they're some kind of treasure?'

'Because they loved their owners, and their owners loved them.'

'Then what about the stuff way over there in the landfill?'

Scrawny's mama turned her dirtied, soot-covered face to look at Bugeye and said coldly, 'That stuff was unloved!'

By the time she was finished, her and Bugeye's hands were completely black with soot. Bugeye felt somehow like he'd just helped a neighbour whom he'd known a long time to move houses. He made up his mind to come back the very next day and place Baldspot's old baseball cap under the shrine as well. After all, the hat that had lost its master must be missing Baldspot, too.

*

Spring came on the wind. The construction of fifty blocks of pre-fabricated buildings was completed in forty days; each block contained twenty-five rooms roughly sixteen square metres in size. Portable public showers also appeared. Bugeye's father, who had been taken away long ago to be schooled on following the straight and narrow, never came back, and a letter arrived from Baron Ashura, who said he was working on the prison sanitation crew. After the shantytown burned down, Scrawny mama's symptoms worsened. She started alarming others not only in the landfill but also in town, and after the management office called in a report, she was taken to a hospital from which she did not re-emerge for the rest of the year. Was it actually possible, Bugeye wondered, for all of those who had left, to return as shiny new people, as if they'd only been taken somewhere to get sprayed down and disinfected? His mother's sole remaining wish was to send Bugeye to school, but he had no intention of finding himself locked up inside a school or prison or hospital or anything of that sort.

After Scrawny's mama left, Bugeye's life grew busier than before. Every day after work, he would gather up any special food that he'd found in the trash, and take it over to Scrawny's house. Peddler Grandpa, who was now living on his own, collected leftover food as well, but at some point the dogs had begun waiting for Bugeye's deliveries instead. Even before he arrived, the members of Scrawny's household knew he was coming, and were already panting and whining. They would all come running the moment he stepped inside, and clamour to be picked up.

One day, after dishing the food out equally to the pups as he always did, Bugeye headed out across the field and over the hill to the hideout. The frequent spring rains had turned the marks left over from the fire a slick black, and the ground was muddy. He sat down in front of the hideout and watched the sun set across the river. It was slowly growing darker when a kind of dark shadow came and sat down quietly next to him. Bugeye turned to look, and there, dressed in grown-up coveralls with the sleeves rolled up and that torn baseball cap perched on his head at an angle, was Baldspot, sitting beside him and gazing out at the same place. Bugeye started to speak, but the boy pointed and whispered, 'There.'

Bugeye saw several blue points of light moving in the darkness down where the river met the foot of the hill. He held his breath as he watched the lights pause and bob and glide along as if dancing. When Bugeye looked back at Baldspot, Baldspot was standing several feet away. Then, like a soap bubble bursting, the shadowy form vanished and became a single blue speck of light that floated down to the bank of the river. For some reason, Bugeye felt like he should apologise, as if he'd done something wrong and shouldn't show his face around those parts again. But then it hit him.

'Oh, thank goodness,' he murmured.

All of this, from the outskirts of the city to the heart of downtown, the countless houses and buildings and automobiles and highways and railroad bridges and street lights and the ear-splitting racket and the vomit on the streets left by drunks and the trash heaps and the discarded things and the dust and the smoke and the rotten smells and every toxic thing, all of these terrible things, were made by the living, by the people of this world. But, with time, the flower stalks would bore their way through the ash of the charred fields and stretch and sway in the wind, tender new leaves would unfurl on the scorched branches, the dark-green blades of young silver grass would slide up from the earth. They would come back. They always had.